N[illegible]

By Lainie Suzanne

Find out more about the author and upcoming books online at www.lainiesuzanne.com

Nexus
ISBN 978-0692240069
Cover Artist: Lainie Suzanne
Published in the United States of America

Acknowledgements

To my Husband, the Love of my Life –
Thank you for your relentless love and support.
You are my beginning and my end.
I love you!

To my Sister – Thank you for taking this journey with me and for your love, encouragement, and unwavering support.
You're the BEST! I love you!

To my dear friend A – Thank you for being my sounding board. I am truly blessed with your friendship. xxxooo

To my Children –
Never stop Dreaming, Never stop believing in yourself.
I love you!

To my family and friends – Thank you for your love, friendship, and support!

Table of Contents

Chapter 1

What a week! No, what a month!!! I think I officially hate March and April. Tax season and working part-time doing tax returns is a nightmare. However, college tuition times two ain't cheap. I would work ten part-time jobs to make sure my boys have a shot at their dream. I guess that's every parent's wish...for their kids to have a better life than they had. Well, most parents anyway. Unfortunately, my boys have an asswipe, sperm donor for a father. A father that walked out of their lives years ago and never looked back.

Miranda Lambert's *Fastest Girl in Town* blaring from my phone, drags me from the reminiscent black hole of my past. *Deb's personal ringtone.*

"Hey Deb, what's up?"

"This is Warden Jenkins, mam. It is April 15th and I'm calling Ms. Katherine Stevens to release her from *tax return prison*," Deb snarks into my ear.

"Why, thank you Warden Jenkins," I chuckle into the phone.

"Seriously Kathy, we need to celebrate!"

"Well, let me remind you *Warden Jenkins* that today is Tuesday. It's 10pm and I have to be at my regular job at 8am in the morning, so no celebrating tonight." *Although, a Margarita with a double shot of tequila sounded great about now.* "We're not in college," I remind her. *When we partied to the wee hours, went to class, went to work, and partied some more; with no sleep. That's been 20 some odd years ago.*

With a heavy sigh, she agrees, "Fine, I'll call you tomorrow and we'll make some plans to celebrate this weekend. And I mean...celebrate!" She grouses with a hint of mischief in her voice.

I relent to her pleas, "Okay."

****

Heels off, bra off...time to relax. No tequila, but a hot bubble bath, glass of wine, and my Kindle will do just fine tonight. Sinking into a steamy heaven, I ponder what to read next.

Scrolling through endless erotic romance books, I land at the one I've read more times than I care to count, *My Liege of Dark Haven* by Cherise Sinclair. God, I love this book. I love Xavier, my favorite *fictional boyfriend*. Fiction...yep, that's what my life has come to. I don't even want to know how much money I've spent on books over the past few years. I would be ashamed, I'm sure. But 1-click is so easy and 3.99 here and there, seems reasonable. Now, nearing two hundred books, I probably need to consider seeking professional help - an intervention maybe; my thoughts as I down my last sip of wine.

It's fucking, Debra's fault - *"Oh my god, Kathy... You have to read Fifty, you just have to."* On and on she went about it, until I finally broke down and bought it. And the rest they say... is history.

Good lord, what reading that book did to me! Debra was constantly saying, *"wait til you get to chapter 7, you're gonna die."*

Well I distinctly remember getting to the infamous chapter seven. I was flying back from a girl's weekend with my sister, on an overbooked flight. As I was reading, a man sitting next to me kept leaning over, peering to see what I was reading. I think he got a glimpse of the book cover when I powered up my Kindle. I leaned into the window for a little privacy, and he leaned over, too. AWKWARD!!! I finished chapter six as we were landing. O M G... I couldn't get off that damn plane fast enough.

Luggage...I need my luggage. I need to get to my car! Throwing my bag in the trunk, I quickly get in my car and power the Kindle on.

I sit in my car at three in the afternoon reading and slowly re-reading chapter 7 and 8. My heart begins to flutter and my panties become damp. Pressure begins to build in my core and my sex throbs. My hand slides down to my mound, my middle finger grazing my clit. My finger continues downward until sliding into the slickness. Drawing my wetness back to my clit, I gently circle the nub, gradually increasing the pressure. My heart begins to pound and I lose focus or care of my surroundings, hell bent on seeking the release I need. My hips grind into my hand giving me the pressure I need on my mound and the friction to my clit. With pounding heart, I clench my eyes as splendor takes over and my release pulsates under my hand. Pulling myself together I drive home.

I finish the series in 2 days and make a trip to the local adult toy store, to purchase my first B.O.B.

Pulling my pruning body from the bath, I collect my Kindle, my vibrator, and take *Xavier* to bed.

Chapter 2

Amazing how good your day starts when you know it's only going to be a nine-hour day instead of fourteen. I stroll through the doors of AMG ~ Atlanta Media Group, caramel mocha in hand.

"Good Morning, Jean. How are you this morning?" I smile to our receptionist, better known as the person who keeps this place running.

"Morning hon, you're looking chipper this morning."

"Tax season is over. My normal life resumes," I rejoice, pumping my fist in the air. I hear Jean cheering as I walk away. Reaching my desk, I quickly put my things away and plunge into reports stacked on my desk.

The twinkle of a text message draws my attention from the ocean of numbers I've been drowning in. Giving my brain a break, I take a look at my phone.

Debra: lunch???

Me: Sure... I should be ready in an hour or so. Is 12 good?

Debra: Umm...it's 11:30 now. Do you mean 12 or 1pm???

Me: WHAT!?!?! I've been buried in reports. The morning has flown by. But yeah, 12 is good.

Debra: Delancy's???

Me: Delancy's @ 12. See ya there!

Delancy's is busy as usual. They have the best subs and freshest salads. I spot Deb waving her arm from the back corner.

"Hey Girlie," I greet, sliding into the booth.

"Hey Chicka," Deb's bubbly voice chirps.

Deb is a petite brunette, olive skin, chocolate brown eyes and a permanent smile; polar opposite of me - tall, plump, auburn hair, grey eyes, fair skin and freckles. Deb's divorced from her high school sweetheart, who I believe still loves her, but he has that fatal flaw of having a wandering eye and wandering hands. He still finds excuses to call her even though they've been divorced for 5 years and have no children. He knows he screwed up the best thing that ever happened to him.

"Soooo..." Deb slurs with an impish grin. "I've been thinking about something different to do this weekend to celebrate your release from *tax return prison*."

"And...," I respond with a raised eyebrow.

Silence fills the air while Deb gathers her thoughts. There's no telling what this crazy woman wants to get into. She looks meek and mild, but looks can be deceiving.

"Well...um, I..."

"For goodness sake Deb, spit it out."

"Well, I was thinking we could go to Nexus," she blurts out with a wicked gleam.

"Come again!" I choke, spewing tea across the table.

"Nexus. They're having their annual open house this Saturday night. I thought it would be awesome for us to go."

"What the hell have you been smokin'? Are you out of your mind?" I shriek. "You do know what Nexus is, don't you?"

"Shhh..., of course I do. It's a BDSM club," she hisses,

darting her eyes around to make sure no one is listening to our conversation.

"So, you are HIGH!"

"*WHAT?!?!* We've read all about the intensely erotic things that go on in these clubs. That's fiction. Don't you want to see for yourself what really and truly goes on?"

Shaking my head, "That's just it, Deb, what we read is FICTION...not real. You have no idea what we would be getting into. It could be dangerous...nasty...filthy," I shiver.

Craning her neck, Deb leans across the table, "I checked into it first, before saying anything to you. It's an upscale place, no riff raff. Tight security inside and out. Besides, this is an open house event so people interested in this lifestyle can get a sneak peek. I'm sure it will be a tame event. Come on...,"

"I'm not going half naked into some strange place. Hell, I'm not half naked in my own apartment most of the time. So, N...,"

"Stop right there," Deb interrupts. "You don't have to be naked. The website said *dressy casual* for the open house. The only stipulation is no jeans and no athletic shoes. So what do ya say? Come on...please???" She begs.

"I don't know, Deb...it's just not me. I'll feel so out of place. Men don't even approach me in a bar. If I go to a BDSM club, they'll be looking at me like, '*what's the chunky chick doing here?'*"

"OH MY GOD, you're the one smokin' crack, Kathy! You are beautiful! Men don't approach you in a bar because they're intimidated by you. They know they don't have a chance in hell with you," she chides.

"Uh...yeah, right!"

"Oh, for fucks sake bitch, you are going and that's the end of it!" She snaps at me.

Rolling my eyes and shaking my head in surrender and defeat. I continue my lunch in silence, pondering who the hell is crazier, Deb for suggesting it or me for allowing myself to be pressured into a nightmare situation. It's a toss-up...we're both insane.

****

Thoughts of what to wear on our venture to Nexus on Saturday filtered through my mind all afternoon. According to Deb, *dressy casual* was allowed for their open house event.

Hmm, Khakis, a Cardigan, and a dungeon... just seems to be something wrong with that picture. It screams ~ *I'm an outsider and a dumbass!*

I definitely don't want to look like I'm there to participate in anything, but I don't want to stick out like a sore thumb.

I seriously need to overcome my growing fear of humiliating myself. But I don't think that's going to happen, seeing as my *self* pep talk is not working. It's a shame they don't sell courage in a bottle. *Well, there is tequila*, I giggle to myself.

After doing a little research and talking to Deb, the next day I make a little trip to the adult *toy* store. I still get embarrassed going inside the store, even though I've been in there half a dozen times. It's a classy store, not sleazy at all. Not only do they have a large variety of novelty items, they have a large selection of lingerie and club attire. With each piece of lacy material that I touch, a new idea for an outfit pops in my head. Over an hour later and lots of help from the salesclerk, I narrow my selection down to two choices. Taking a deep breath, I close my eyes and make my final selection. With my outfit planned, I head home.

Chapter 3

Strips of sunlight through the blinds make mini rainbows across my bed, stirring me awake as they make their way upon my face. I lay peacefully making a mental list of things I need to do today. A trip to the grocery store, pay bills, laundry... OH MY GOD, IT'S SATURDAY!!! We're going to Nexus... TONIGHT!!! The thought catapults me upright, as realization registers in my brain and panic begins to seize my heart.

Scratch the previous mental list and focus on the new one... Manicure, pedicure; shave - legs, underarms, groom bikini area. *Do I really need to groom my bikini area? Who the hell's gonna see it, much less touch it?* I think to myself. *Better to be safe than sorry...no make that, more embarrassed,* I rationalize and keep grooming on my list.

I spend the afternoon pampering and primping myself. The knot in my stomach starts to grow as each hour passes. Doubt swirls through my head. I must be out of my mind for even considering going to a BDSM club. It's no place for me. I read erotic romance...I don't live it. *Yes, reading erotica does stir wondrous feelings inside me. Yes, I get aroused reading; at times needing to relieve the pressure that builds between my legs, but that doesn't mean I need to go dive head first into a BDSM club,* I reason, desperately trying to convince myself I should stay home.

Miranda Lambert's voice draws me out of my thoughts...I grab my phone.

"Hey Deb," I draw out trying to sound tired. *Yeah, I'm tired; may be coming down with something, that's what I'll tell her. Probably best if I stay home.*

"DON'T EVEN THINK ABOUT BAILING ON ME!" Deb growls, as she enunciates each word with punctuation. *How the hell do you growl and enunciate at the same time?*

"BAIL...me??? No way! What makes you think I'm gonna bail?" I quip, rolling my eyes. *I really can't disappoint her like that. She went to a lot of trouble to plan this night out for me, thinking it would be something I would like. I need to suck it up, put my big girl panties on and try to have a good time.*

"Umm o-kaaay..., she says skeptically. I was calling to let you know I'll be over around 8:30."

"Great, I'll be ready. Just plan to stay here tonight. I'm sure we will have lots to talk about when we get home."

"Sounds good. See ya soon," Deb replies as she hangs up.

****

I pull into the driveway of a beautiful, plantation style home. Huge Oak trees encase the entrance to the home. I slow to a stop.

"Are you sure you typed the correct address in the GPS?" I ask. "This is someone's home. I don't see any other cars. I need to turn around somehow. That's all I need is to be seen by *The Jones* in a corset, skirt, and thigh high boots," I ramble on, scanning the surroundings from side to side.

"Hold on, let me double check to make sure. Yep...this is it Kathy."

"Are you sure? I see lights on, but where are the other cars? Are you certain tonight is the Open House? Maybe we got the date wrong," I shrug.

"No, it's tonight, I double checked that too, when I rechecked the address."

I continue down the long drive. As I approach, what is clearly a mansion, I notice a small sign directing me to the parking area behind the house. Sure enough, there is a large parking area and it's almost full. I find a spot and park.

With a deep breath I open my car door and make my way out, struggling to keep from showing my ass to anyone standing around. Deb comes around the car as I'm tucking and adjusting my goodies in this corset. It is a beautiful corset; a royal, majestic purple satin bodice with lacings; coupled with a black silk blend skirt resting mid-thigh. I broke the bank adding in the black thigh-high pleather boots. But it all seems to have really worked together to camouflage this plump body. My tummy rolls are cinched snug to my torso, the skirt covers my thick hips and round ass. The boots cover the majority of my legs, so bare skin is at a minimal. The only other major flaw not concealed is my flabby upper arms. Ick!!! My goodies are just sitting on a display shelf, not really restricted in any way. But as long as I don't go flappin' my arms like a chicken or bending over in any way, I should be okay.

"Damn, girl...You look HOT! I've never seen you dress this way! All PURPLICIOUS!" sassed Deb.

"Umm...no, you haven't 'cause I've never been to a BDSM club before. And you look pretty HOT yourself. Did you paint that little yellow dress on?" I giggle. "It's snugging every curve you have."

"Curves?!?! Girl, please. While everybody else is killing mosquitos, I'm catching them to put on my chest to bite, so I have some tits," Deb says rolling her eyes.

I'm laughing so hard my goodies are about to escape. Taking a deep breath to calm my laughter, I take a last look down, making sure all the curves and rolls have remained intact.

"All right, Deb...let's do this!"

We make our way to the entrance, where I notice a small, elegant, brass plate with NEXUS engraved. Just inside the door we are greeted by a twenty-something, platinum blonde, wearing a red leather bra and matching thong.

"Welcome to Nexus!" shrills the blonde bombshell. "Are you here for the Open House Event?"

"Yes," Deb confirms her question.

"Great! What name is your reservation under?"

"Debra Jenkins and Katherine Stevens," Deb replies.

Blondie scans a list, "Ah, there you are. You ladies

snagged two of the last spots. It still amazes me how fast these reservations go. We've been booked over two months."

Two months??? What in the...that little sneak. I'm gonna kill her.

"Yes... we were lucky," Deb mumbles, as she avoids my glare at her.

"Let me get the rules and consent forms you need to sign."

As she's gathering papers, I firmly grab Deb's elbow, turning her toward me.

"Two months, you little sneak... you've been planning this for two months!?!?" I grouse through clenched teeth.

"What difference does it make if I planned it two months or two days ago? We're here and that's all that matters."

I give her my patented, '*you're gonna pay for this'* look, as Blondie begins explaining the papers we're about to sign.

"Please read the rules and follow them. The Dungeon Monitors have zero-tolerance for broken rules."

Dungeon Monitor, WTH???

"Excuse me." I interrupt. "What's a *Dungeon Monitor*?"

"They are members of the staff trained in BDSM safety techniques. They observe all scenes and insure the safety of everyone. You can recognize them by the red Nexus vest they wear. The house safe words; Green – all good; Yellow – pause, slow down, adjust scene; Red – STOP immediately. Dungeon Monitors will respond immediately to Red. They also observe scenes in private rooms. There's a window in the door allowing them to see and hear. By signing below, you agree that you make your own decisions concerning scenes while remaining within the parameters of the House Rules. You must play Safe, Sane, and Consensual," Blondie concludes.

"We don't plan to participate, just observe. Do we still need to sign consent forms?" I ask.

"No one goes beyond this area without signing them. Besides, you never know when you may see something you want to try," Blondie teases.

"She's right. You never know what might turn you on," this warm, resonant voice suggests. Turning toward the voice so low, it was almost a growl, my eyes fall upon an absolute Adonis.

I'm frozen, gaping mouth, wide eyes... soaking up every ounce of him. Towering around 6' 3", wearing black slacks, black dress shirt - barely containing his brawny physique, with the top 2 buttons undone. The rugged, chiseled features of his face surrounded by short, chestnut colored hair with a sprinkling of grey at his temple. I think if he smiles, he will have a dimple within that 5 o'clock shadow outlining his strong jawline.

I'm so awestruck, I can't compose a thought to reply. So I just stand there.

Finally, Deb nudges my arm and I utter something...I think I said "You're right", but more like "Uh, huh", like a babbling fool. Whatever I said, Mr. Adonis found it amusing, because he smiles. And I was right...Dimples.

DAMN...!!!

Chapter 4

With papers signed and a bright, red wristband placed snuggly around my wrist; I drag myself from the hypnotic allure of *Dimples,* and Deb and I make our way through the lobby into a world unknown to me.

The light, woodsy smell of leather and musk invade my senses. A pulsating rhythm surrounds me as we enter through the double doors; loud, but not deafening. The lyrics sound like a cadence, making them almost garbled, but I faintly hear the *"...Voodoo, Voodoo..."* and I believe it's Godsmack. *I recognize it from thumping through the boys' walls when they're home.* The music is laced with moaning undertones, accentuated with pleading cries, moans, and tears. I tap down my immediate curiosity to locate the sounds adjoining the music.

I'm trying hard not to appear like a gawking tourist, as I subtly scan the open area. There's a bar to my immediate right, where stools and tables are filled with people laughing and chatting, like at any other bar. There's a small dance floor directly in front of us, and beside the bar. There are few people on the dance floor, the music is not the dancing kind. However, there's a couple in the middle of the dance floor; the man looks to be in his forties – shirtless, wearing black jeans and boots. The woman appears to be in her late twenties – wearing a hot pink top made of netting; similar to a swimsuit cover, and nothing more. On his knees, the man has a firm grip on the woman's hips, running his tongue between her folds, as she groans out her pleasure.

I turn to check Deb's reaction; her chin is resting on her chest; her eyes are the size of saucers.

I nudge her shoulder, "let's get a drink," I start to say, changing my mind mid-sentence. "How about a bottle water, instead? I don't think I want to be under the influence of anything tonight. I want to keep what wits I have intact."

Deb agrees and we make our way to the bar.

Taking a sip of water to quench my dry throat, the crack of a whip resonates through the air, startling us both, causing me to slosh water onto my chest. The sudden chill is actually refreshing and awakens me from succumbing to this mesmeric feeling.

I'm drawn toward my left, in the direction of the

cracking sound. We walk over and stand behind a small gathering of people; a vast, mahogany cross comes into view. *It's beautiful.* A *St. Andrew's cross,* I assume. I recognize it from the descriptions in the books I've read.

A woman leans, vulnerable and naked against the cross, wrists and ankles shackled; one at each corner of the cross. A bald man, dressed in black, stands behind her inspecting...no, more like admiring the crimson design on her back. He takes several steps back, brandishing the whip, once again. After a pregnant pause, the crack of the whip blasts through the silence, a shiver ripping through me as another fiery ribbon adorns the woman's back. I hear a subtle moan escape her lips. Her body loses its form when her legs buckle beneath her. *Snap..., crack..., snap, again!* The intricate pattern on her back expands. He winds the whip around his hand and reattaches it to his belt. I exhale the breath I didn't realize I was holding, as he approaches the shackled woman. He hovers at her ear and appears to whisper something to her. He nuzzles the nape of her neck, placing small kisses along the way; at the same time, he reaches up, freeing her wrists. He brings his arms around her, filling his right hand with her taut breast and his left cups her sex, all while his tongue explores her mouth. He pulls his middle finger between her folds, and then into his mouth. He proceeds to unshackle her ankles, quickly wrapping her in a blanket and gathers her in his arms. I catch a glimpse of the expression on her face, leaving no doubt to her enamored state. I'm shocked at my own arousal at their display, as dampness spreads between my legs.

The small crowd disperses and Deb and I begin to make our way to the left. I discreetly observe my surroundings as we proceed deeper into the club. There are people in varying styles of clothing, as well as amounts of clothing or lack thereof. Approaching us, a younger man, appearing to be in his late 20's or early 30's, is being led around by a leash attached to a thick leather collar around his neck. He is crawling on his hands and knees and wearing what appears to be a jock strap of some sort. A petite, beautiful woman in her late 30's, dressed in black leather from head to toe, is holding the leash. She stops just in front of us. I suddenly feel a little apprehensive. *Was I staring too overtly? Am I supposed to avoid looking at him?*

"Welcome to Nexus! My name is Charlotte," the woman's greeting interrupts my thoughts. "Is this your first time visiting?"

"Thank you, Charlotte! I'm Katherine and this is Debra. Nice to meet you," I nod, not sure if extending my hand is appropriate here. "Yes, this is our first time visiting. It's a beautiful place." I'm trying desperately not to stare at the man at my feet.

"This is my sub Edward. Edward, please rise and greet these lovely ladies and welcome them," she utters with a gentle tug on the leash.

Edward rises and I mean *rises*, over six foot, completely towering over Charlotte. My eyes run the length of his torso. He is a gorgeous specimen. *Holy shit...what is that between his legs. That is no jock strap that I've ever seen.* He reaches for Deb's hand, placing a chaste kiss on her hand. Gently releasing Deb's hand, he extends an offer to take mine, bringing it to his luscious, thick lips.

"Welcome ladies," oozes like molasses from those lips.

Dear god...I could listen to him say that over and over and soak my panties; without him laying a finger on me. Charlotte's eyes direct Edward back to the floor with a slight nod. Immediately he resumes his previous position on the floor, lowering his head further to plant a kiss on both of her shiny leather boots.

Guess I was staring again, as Charlotte's voice brings me back to the here and now, "... if you have any questions, just ask anyone. We're all pretty friendly."

I miss the first part of what she was saying, but acknowledge with a smile, thanking her, as they walk and uh, crawl away.

"What the FUCK is he wearing?!?!" Deb gasps, pulling on my arm. "It looks like a fucking cage for his...COCK!!!"

"Maybe it's like a chastity belt, but for men," I guess. "I was wondering the same thing, trying not to gawk at it, when he stood up."

Shaking her head, Deb tugs my elbow and we continue, stopping at a couple more scenes. There are several tables set up along the hall with information ranging from BDSM basics, Safety, Bondage, Shibari, Caning, and Lifestyle etiquette. Each table has someone there knowledgeable in that specific area that you can talk to and demonstrations are being offered in some. Deb actually signs up for the bondage demo they're having later on tonight.

We stop at the flogging information table. *I am fascinated with flogging, mostly because of the books I've read. The erotic and sensual way they are described in my favorite stories has me secretly dreaming about experiencing it myself. But that's where it will remain, in my dreams...a fantasy. I certainly do not like pain of any kind, sexual or not.* The man, who I assume is the expert flogger, is well into his discussion of flogging techniques. Deb and I, both pick up pamphlets and begin perusing through them.

"You ladies interested in flogging?" asks a raspy voice, with just a hint of an accent. Looking up, my eyes are treated to *Tall, Dark, and Sexy*.

"Uhhh..." *I don't know what to say...*

"I'm Patrick, I'm a Dungeon Master here at Nexus. Welcome!"

Dungeon Master...is that different from a Dungeon Monitor???

"So... being that you're here, I'm going to make a leap of faith that you have some realm of interest in BDSM; more specifically...flogging. Am I correct?" He surmises. His voice laced with the accent I'm trying to place.

I steal a glance at Deb and she is beet red. I feel the warming sensation of my own embarrassment creeping up my chest and neck.

"Y-yes...yes, I do." I murmur, dropping my gaze to the floor. *Why the hell did I say that?*

"No need to be embarrassed...," He places his finger under my chin, lifting my face back to his.

"Katherine and this is my friend, Debra," I finish his sentence.

"Great to meet you, ladies. So Katherine, where did your interest begin?"

"Um...well...books" I confess and immediately dart my eyes to the floor, once again. *Why the fuck did I say THAT? Jeezus...what is wrong with me?*

Patrick chuckles under his breath, as he lifts my chin a second time.

"We all get our interest from somewhere and there's certainly no shame in getting it from a book" his brilliant smile beaming at me.

I glance around at Deb to make sure she's still standing there, because she is making no sound whatsoever. *Bitch...ditching me in this conversation.* OH MY GOD... that's when I see him, standing off to the side behind Patrick. *It's my Adonis! No... not mine, I remind myself.* My God...he is SEXY!!! I don't see the dimples now. He has that - *don't fuck with me* - look on his face. He doesn't look mean, just deep in thought. *Besides, you would have to be crazy to mess with him.* I'm drinking in every drop of his deliciousness, from his thick muscular legs all the way up to his sexy ... Oh, SHIT!!!

He caught me staring at him. I quickly look away, hoping he was looking past me.

Patrick interrupts my delicious thoughts - "There's a flogging demonstration later tonight. You should sign up."

"Me??? No, thank you."

"Oh, come now Katherine. Here's your chance to experience it within a safe environment, by someone that is specially trained. Tell her Debra. That is your name, isn't it, *Sweetheart*?" his sultry voice hypnotizing us both. "You've been awfully quiet," he continues, stroking her body with his gaze.

I bet everyman in here has checked Deb out? She looks like she's been dipped in yellow latex, the way her dress is formed to her body. Still, Deb stands there, dumbstruck, not saying a word. Patrick lets out another little chuckle. Seems we're his amusement for the night.

"Thank you for the offer, but I must decline. Maybe next time," I offer. *Next time??? What the hell am I saying??? We need to move on before my mouth gets us in a mess.*

Pulling Deb from her stupor, I lead her away from the hypnotic trance of *Tall, Dark, and Sexy* and myself away from the delectable sight of *Adonis*.

"What do you mean leaving me hanging like that?" I hiss. "I wanted to dig a hole and bury myself and you just stand there with drool puddling at your feet."

"I'm sorry, I don't know what's wrong with me. I couldn't tear my eyes away from his or make a sound come from my lips. But DAMN...he is sexy as fuck!"

Laughing out, I agree with her assessment.

Chapter 5

We continue our venture around the club. I notice a few more red wrist bands, but seriously, you just have to look at the expressions on faces. You definitely know who the visitors, *more like voyeurs*, are. The visitors could care less who the other visitors are, but we clearly stick out to the regulars.

We pass several scenes, stopping at each to get a better look. In one scene, a young woman was wrapped in rope from her hips to her shoulders, with her arms completely enveloped and immobile. She was suspended several feet off the ground, in a prone position, face down. An older man, I'm guessing in his 70's, though he looks to be in great shape, has a hand under each of her thighs; maneuvering her back, at the same time thrusting his cock into her sex. She is writhing and crying out with every pleasurable thrust.

As I watch, pressure starts to rise low in my belly and the pulsing begins in my sex. I never thought I could be turned on watching complete strangers have sex. I must have checked every ounce of dignity I had at the door, because I clearly have none, standing here being aroused watching this erotic scene.

An announcement comes through the speakers stating the bondage demonstration will begin shortly. We make our way to the designated area, where a crowd is beginning to form. A gorgeous man, with skin the color of delicious caramel, stands before us with a million-dollar smile, a gleam in his eye, and rope in his hand. He introduces himself as Master Derek and begins explaining different forms of bondage techniques – rope harness, honor bondage, suspension bondage, Shibari; bondage positions – kneeling, lotus, mummification *~WTF is that;* and bondage equipment – cuffs, spreader bar, St. Andrew's Cross, straitjacket - *holy hell.*

He begins calling people up to demonstrate. Debra's name is called and she bolts over to *Mr. Delicious*, I mean Master Derek. I can't believe she is going through with this. She is nuts!

Minimal words are exchanged between Deb and Master *Delicious*, that no one can hear, and she's quickly placed in a kneeling position. Her wrists are tied behind her, at her waist. He gently lowers her completely to the floor. I try to see her expression, but most of her face is covered by her hair. He skillfully binds her ankles to her wrists, opening her completely to him.

"This is the *Lotus* position," he announces. He gently strokes his finger up her spine. Deb finally moves her head, hair falling away from her face, and I see the arousal in her eyes.

He unfastens her restraints, gently rubbing her wrists and ankles as he examines them carefully. Again, a brief exchange of words and he helps her to her feet, before lifting her hand to his lips. And there it is again...that dumbstruck look on her face. I giggle to myself.

"That was AMAZING!!! He smells so good. His hands were so strong, yet so gentle. I so wanted him to thrust his cock in me. Does that make me a slut? Hell...I don't care if it does. I'll be a slut...his slut!" Deb babbles on.

I just smile, nod, shake my head, and desperately try not to bust out laughing.

"I need a drink..." She asserts.

We walk back to the bar and Deb orders a seven & seven and I get a bottle water. We find a table near the dance floor and sit down to people watch for a bit. As eccentric and diverse as everyone here is, they are all very friendly and welcoming. Lots of smiles and offers to answer any questions we may have. I guzzle my water, not realizing how thirsty I really was.

Frankie Goes to Hollywood is pumping through the speakers and I'm in full-on chair dancing mode; rockin' my hips, swaying my arms, really grooving – all while sitting in my chair. I love music and I love to dance. So when I hear a good beat, I can't help but move. After several chair-groovin' songs; slow, background music starts to play. Our chair dancing has worked up a thirst, so I go to retrieve round two of our drinks. While waiting for the bartender, I hear the warm, resonant voice that captivated my attention when we first arrived. Inconspicuously, I glance to my left and I see him...*Adonis,* talking to the blond bombshell that was at the door when we came in. They must be a couple. *When I first saw Adonis, he was up front talking to her, now he's at the bar talking to her. He must've been waiting for her to get off work. She looks a little young for him, but who am I kidding. That's what all men my age want...a younger woman. Oh shit...the bartender needs to hurry and bring the drinks before Adonis notices me. He's gonna think I'm a freaking stalker.*

I get our drinks and head back to the table.

I shove Deb's drink at her, "Slam it, chick! We need to

mosey on away from this area. *Adonis* over there has caught me staring at him twice. I don't want him to think I'm a creeper. He's over there talking to his woman," I toss my head in their direction. Just then, an announcement blares through the speaker, stating the Flogging Demonstration is about to begin.

We make our way to the designated area for the flogging demo. I blush when I see Patrick, recalling our interrogating conversation about my interest in flogging. I momentarily consider not watching the demo to avoid further embarrassment...but, I'm really excited about watching it in person. My curiosity has been piqued.

Patrick begins talking about floggers, Cat o' nines, Quirts, and whips. I'm mesmerized by each instrument he holds up, completely blocking out his descriptions and explanations. My attention is drawn to the St. Andrew's cross erected behind Patrick. It's rich, mahogany wood has intricate detailing at each point. It is stunning. I've read so much about them in books, but it's still quite overwhelming in person.

Patrick calls several people up for demos. It's like I'm in a dream. It's so erotic watching someone feel the flogger at their back.

"Katherine Stevens ..."

Deb nudges my arm, “He’s calling your name.”

“What? Who?” I stammer.

“Patrick...he’s calling you to come up there. I didn’t think you signed up,” she says quizzically.

“I DIDN’T!”

Patrick is standing in front of me with his hand held out. “Come on Katherine, don’t be shy,” he coaxes.

“Uh... I think there’s been a mistake. I didn’t sign up for a demo,” continuing to shake my head in disbelief.

Patrick looks at a paper on a clipboard. “*Katherine Stevens*...it’s right here on the list. That’s your name, isn’t it?”

“Yes, that’s my name, but I didn’t sign up. There’s been a mistake.”

“Hon, your name is on my list. You’re not gonna get me in trouble with the boss, are you?” He asks, a wicked grin emerging on his lips.

“Go ahead, Kathy. You’ll be fine. It’s a dream come true for you,” Deb urges me on.

“Are you crazy? I’m not going up there and let some stranger whip me. You’ve lost your mind!”

Overhearing our conversation, Patrick steps closer, stroking the flogger up and down my arm. It feels so soft with the potential for pain clearly hidden.

"I promise I won't hurt you. Well, unless you want me to," he whispers into my ear, winking as he pulls away.

"You can do this!" Deb cheers.

My eyes shooting daggers at Deb, I reluctantly place my hand in the one Patrick is holding out to me.

Not only do I hear my heart pounding in my ears, I can feel it. Patrick leads me over to the beautiful cross. *What the fuck am I doing?* He guides me to where I'm facing the cross, so close that the earthy smell of the wood transcends my senses. He's whispering calming sounds, saying words I'm sure, but my fear and excitement have entwined, preventing me from focusing clearly. Patrick attaches the restraints to my wrists and ankles, bound and at his mercy. His soothing voice instructs me to close my eyes and take some slow, deep breaths, as he assures me of my safety once again.

My peace is interrupted when the leather strands softly caress my back, while warm breath at my right ear growls my name. OH MY GOD...it's him. It's *Adonis*

Chapter 6

"What's going on? Who are you?" I murmur, knowing damn well who it is but too scared to see for sure.

"I didn't say you could speak sub," growls that voice, *his* voice.

Sub...What the FUCK is going on?

"I'm not a sub, there's been some mistake," I try to assert, but fail miserably.

"Right now, you ARE a sub, MY sub...for the duration of this scene," he continues growling into my ear.

A shiver bolts down my spine; spreading chills in its wake, my nipples hardening to attention - all with the sound of *his* voice. My body is frozen, but my mind is racing. *What the hell is going on? Scene...what scene??? I'm not in a scene and I'm certainly not in a scene with HIM. Why is he here? Where is Patrick? What the fuck is going on?*

I feel myself beginning to panic and I take a deep breath to try and calm my nerves. *His* voice interrupts my thoughts.

"That's it, take a deep breath. No need to panic, Katherine."

He said my name again. God I love hearing him say it.

"Master Patrick needed to attend to something, so I'm finishing his demonstration. My name is Master Isaac."

Mmmm, Master Isaac...

"Master Patrick is an expert on flogging," I state turning my head to try to get a glimpse of him. "I'm not sure I'm comfortable with you flogging me. I don't know your credentials. Are you an expert, too?" I ask a little teasingly.

Not that I really care if he's an expert. I'm just trying to even the playing field a bit. Feeling his chest against my back, I hear a small grunt of a laugh as he leans down to my ear again.

"Being that I trained Master Patrick, I'm fairly confident I have the credentials to flog you, sub. Shall we continue?"

I reply with a nod and a breathless, "yes."

Again, he starts stroking the top of my back with the

soft strands of leather. It feels amazing, relaxing every muscle it caresses. I close my eyes enjoying the languor. Once again his voice pulls me back...

"To experience the true effects of the flogger, it must strike the skin directly. You have too much covered, something needs to go. I choose the skirt," he declares.

My eyes flash open...*did I hear him, right? Does he want to take my skirt off?* My questions are answered as I feel his hands at my waist.

"WHOA...wait a minute!!!" *Colors... What are the fucking colors???* "YELLOW, RED, PURPLE ...WHATEVER! Don't take my skirt off!!! No, no...NO!!!"

"Purple???" He snickers.

"I'm sorry, I don't know what I'm doing, but please, please, please don't take my skirt off."

He steps around and I get my first look into his warm, chestnut eyes that match his hair. *My knees slightly give...God, he's beautiful*!

"The safe word colors are green, yellow, and red. Green, all is good. Yellow, slow down or you need a break. Red, everything stops immediately. You have the control,

Katherine. Do you understand?" He's looking so deep into my eyes; I believe he can see my soul.

I blink to break his intense gaze, as I feel like I'm revealing more than I care to and I nod my head in answer to his question.

"No Katherine, I need a verbal response."

Taking a deep breath, I reply, "Yes."

"Yes, what?" He chides.

"Yes Sir."

Stepping out of my sight, he takes his hand over my ample ass, resting it on my left cheek. "I want to flog your ass and I want it bare."

My breath hitches as his hand wanders under my skirt and caresses my skin. *Oh my god... What am I doing allowing this man that I don't know, to place his hand on my bare ass? Shouldn't I stop this??? Color, color...fuck the colors. I don't want to stop this.* My body is trembling; I know he can feel it.

"How are you, Katherine?" He asks, as if reading my mind.

What do I say? He's gonna think I'm easy...a whore, if

I don't stop him. I don't want to stop him. It's been so long... My body betrays me and answers him, as I let out a weak moan. No doubt he heard, as I hear him let out a small chuckle.

I feel his hands back on my waist at the top of my skirt.

"Please, not the skirt...," I whine.

He steps back around in my view. *Hmmm, maybe I'll keep complaining so I can keep looking at him. Doubt that will last, though.*

"Why do you not want your skirt removed?"

Duh, you're a stranger and GORGEOUS. And I'm pleasantly plump with extra helpings.

"I-I...umm"

"All right, then the corset comes off," He interrupts, as if it's a normal, everyday request.

"No, no, no!!!" I plea shaking my head.

Oh, Hell NO!!! All my tucks will unroll for the world to see. No way!

"What's the issue? We can discuss it, but it's going to be one or the other - skirt, corset, or safeword?"

I drop my gaze as I can't look him in the eyes. I'm so embarrassed. Can't he see...I'm not a young, skinny thing like the blonde bombshell at the door? *Where is she anyway? I thought she was his woman. Hell if I would let my man put his hand on another woman's ass.*

"I'm waiting...," he states firmly.

Taking a deep breath, I steady my nerves and just say it...

"Master Isaac, I'm not young and skinny. I'm middle aged and plump with rolls screaming to get out of this corset. I don't want to be humiliated. I don't even know how my name was put on the list," I wearily confess.

"Are you finished?" He snarls. "I have perfect vision, sub. Now, I gave you a choice, something I rarely do. Either the skirt comes off so I can see your luscious ass, your corset comes off and I flog those delicious looking tits, or you use your safeword. Which is it going to be?" His growl at my neck soaking my panties.

I'll never see him or these people again, and I soooo want this now. What the hell...

"The skirt, Sir."

"Good Girl..."

****

With both hands at my waist, he pulls my skirt down until I feel it at my ankles. He taps each ankle, and I lift each foot to remove the skirt completely. Then he gently lowers my black lace panties, repeating the same process as with the skirt.

He's at my neck and whispers, "I love black lace."

I hear him inhale a deep breath.

"Mmmm...You smell so good." He groans. "Your ass is beautiful, Katherine. Soft and round. I can't wait to pinken that fair skin up. But this will be just a demo, nothing harsh. You have your safeword. Are you ready, Katherine?"

"Yes, Sir." I reply.

I feel him step away and I miss his touch. *Miss his touch...Good god, girl. Get a grip.* I feel the first lash on my right cheek and then my left, right cheek, then left...thud, thud...thud, thud. It feels unbelievably good. He soon sets a rhythm - swack, swack; swack swack... slowly increasing the intensity. It's beginning to sting a tiny bit. Suddenly I feel a tingling sensation throughout my body. My sex is beginning to pulse and is quenched with my essence.

The calming thuds stop and I feel hands rubbing, caressing my ass radiating a warmth throughout my body.

"Good Girl" whispered by *Adonis*, aka Master Isaac into my ear, furthers the warming sensation.

I vaguely realize my hands are free and someone, I assume Master Isaac, is freeing my ankles. A warm blanket is placed around my shoulders and Master Isaac guides to me a plush chaise in the corner. He gently places me on the lounger, sits down beside me and begins examining my ankles and wrists.

"How do you feel? Do you have any tingling or numbness in your extremities?" He asks genuinely concerned.

"I'm good...really good." I mumble, as he continues softly rubbing my wrists.

He begins to inquire about my experience with the events tonight, when blond bombshell appears, apologizing as she interrupts us, saying there's a matter at the front desk that needs his attention.

“Are you sure you’re good?” He asks handing me a bottle of water. I acknowledge I am, as he stands.

“Thank you for the demonstration, Master Isaac. You literally made one of my dreams come true,” I laugh.

“My pleasure, Katherine,” He says placing a light kiss on my forehead. “I need to see to this matter up front. Here’s your skirt. Make sure to see me before you leave.”

Stunned... I smile and nod as he walks away.

I’m fumbling with my skirt when Deb walks up.

“OH MY GOD, Kathy. That was freakin’ HOT!!!” She shrills as she takes my shoulders, shaking me.

“Mmmm, yeah, it was intense,” I vaguely respond as I continue looking around on the floor.

“What are you looking for?”

“My panties...I’m looking for my panties.”

****

Isaac

DAMN GINA and her interruptions. It's probably best, though. I can see things gettin' a little out of hand with that sexy red head. *Katherine Stevens... damn, when I first saw her and those beautiful tits, surrounded by black lace, sitting there on display; I wanted her hard nubs between my teeth. Pulling my glare up to her lips, I wanted to suck on that plump lip she was nervously biting. Definitely not sure she wanted to be here, 'do I have to sign a consent, if I'm not going to participate' - Hell yeah, I knew right then, she would participate one way or another. Then my eyes locked on hers, damn what color are they; green, gray? I want to stare deep into those eyes, drowning in them as I drown my cock in her wet pussy. Fuck...where did that come from???*

But Damn, I didn't want to just pinken that luscious ass, I want it RED. I want it red, by my hand, across my lap. *Shit man, get a grip...*

"What's the problem, Gina?" I ask as we approach the lobby.

"Several member passes were declined tonight. I didn't know if it's a glitch in the system or what? They're regulars, so I let them in and told them I would speak to you to find out what the problem is and told them to see me before they leave," Gina explains.

"Shit! They probably sent a check in for their membership dues, instead of paying online. I have a stack of payments by check that haven't been entered. Online payments update in the system automatically, checks have to be updated manually. I'll take care of it."

"Master Isaac, are you going to hire someone to help out?" She asks cautiously. "I would help out if I could, but I'm horrible at math and worse with a computer."

"Don't worry, Gina, I'll get it taken care of," I respond trying not to sound harsh.

It's not Gina's fault, it's mine. I've put it off long enough. Mrs. Glancey had her heart attack 6 months ago. She refuses to retire, though she's past 70, claiming I need her to run the business efficiently. She's so freakin' stubborn, but she's right...I do need her. She's a little dynamo. I did assert my Dom-ness, by only allowing her to do the books for the construction company. Running the office for the construction company and doing the accounting for the club, was too much for her. Problem is, I don't have time to do the books, either. And there lies the problem...

"Gina, I'll be in my office working on catching this stuff

up. Before the members that had issues leave, find me so I can apologize personally," I call out, heading to my office.

Chapter 7

After pulling myself together and putting my skirt back on, sans my panties, we continue our venture through Nexus. Thankfully, the crowd that gathered to watch the flogging demo, had dispersed. I don't think I could face anyone.

We make our way to the last display table - MEMBERSHIP.

"No need wasting our time here," I declare.

"Ah, come on, let's just check it out...you know, for kicks and giggles," Deb says, pulling me toward the table. Rolling my eyes, we head over.

Skimming over the pamphlet, I notice there are different membership levels, depending on services, facility access, and instruction.

"Holy shit...basic membership is $500 a month!!!" exclaims Deb.

"I see that. I told you there was no need to come over here."

"Damn, who in the hell can afford to be a member here?"

"Not us," I smirk. "Come on, I think we've seen all there is to see."

Making our way back through the club, I ponder what *Adonis*, I mean Master Isaac meant by *'make sure to see him before I leave'? Does he really want me to find him before I leave? Surely not. Why would he? He was probably just making small talk.* As we approach the lobby, I see him on the other side. Thankfully, he's deep in conversation with a gentleman and doesn't notice me. Awkward situation... avoided! We quickly sign out, making our way home.

Dear lord...every fat roll is screaming for joy and my feet are sighing relief. Corset, skirt, and boots off...a hot shower, my sweats and t-shirt on and glass of wine in hand. I plop on the sofa, turning toward Deb at the other end.

"So...what did ya think?" Deb inquires hesitantly.

"I thought it was great, quite fascinating. Thanks for planning it. I know I wasn't too receptive in the beginning, but I really had a great time."

“I did too. No wonder we don’t see hot guys when we go out, they’re all at Nexus,” she chuckles.

“Oh YES… Master Patrick, Master Derek, and Master Isaac…Good LORD they are SEXY HOT!!! You helped make my fantasy come true, girlie. I still can’t figure out how my name got put on that list. So weird…but I’m so happy it did. I can’t put into words the feeling of having Master Isaac’s hands on me, looking into his eyes, and then to actually be flogged by him. Completely UN-BE-LIEVABLE!!!” I marvel. “And my panties, what happened to my panties? Do you think he kept them? Surely not…” I babble on.

“It’s possible. Let me just say that from what I witnessed, your Master Isaac looked to be enjoying himself too,” Deb surmises.

“Nah… I’m sure that was routine for him.”

****

Isaac

After some quiet time in my office, I was able to get a lot of the paperwork caught up, at least the member dues. I apologized to the members whose accounts were blocked and squared things away with them. Maybe if I do this regularly, I can stay caught up and I won't need to find someone to help out around here. *Fuck that... I'd never have time to enjoy my own club*. Finding someone to help out moves to the top of the 'To Do list'.

Damn, it's almost closing time. I was hoping to coax that red headed vixen into a little more play time. I head out of the office and back to the desk in the lobby, where Derek seems to be holding down the fort.

"Hey Derek...Great exhibition tonight. Man, thanks for helping out with open house," I praise, shaking his hand.

"Anytime Isaac. I enjoy introducing people to the life," he grins.

"So, where's Gina? She's supposed to be covering the desk," I ask, just as she comes around the corner.

"Sorry, Sir. After three bottles of water, I couldn't wait any longer," she winces.

"I understand. Just make sure the desk is covered by a staff member before leaving it," I remind her.

Gina has a problem wandering away from the desk when she's on duty, leaving it unattended. She recently received a final reminder about her duty, which is in lieu of her membership dues.

"How many are left in the club?" I call out.

"There are 10 left, all in scenes," Patrick states as he comes around the corner.

"Good, thanks Patrick."

"By the way Gina, did the red head in the purple corset leave? I think her friend was wearing a yellow...something, I don't know. They were guests for the open house," I ramble on. *What the fuck is wrong with me??? Babbling like a pansy bitch.*

"Yes, Sir. They signed out a little before one o'clock, Sir."

Huh, I'm usually pretty good at gauging someone's interest in BDSM, and I thought she was interested. I even told her to see me before she left. Guess she wasn't that interested after all.

I head to the locker room to shower. Forgetting that I kept her lacy panties, I'm pleasantly surprised to find them in my back pocket. Standing under the water, my cock immediately hardens as I replay the scene with her in my head. I reach for her panties on top of the shower wall, inhaling her sweet scent, stroking my swollen cock until it erupts.

****

Each strike lands on alternating cheeks, with more bite than the previous. My sex is so wet, throbbing with need. The lashes stop, his hand rubbing my ass and the warmth radiates to my clit. His finger traces the crevice between my cheeks, delving in as he journeys downward. The tip of his finger grazing over the tight entrance to my forbidden zone. He continues leisurely toward my sex...I'm trembling with anticipation. It's been so long...I need this.

"Master Isaac...PLEASE, please!" His finger stopping.

"Please what, baby?"

"Please fuck me! I can't wait any longer," I plea.

He brushes his finger across my clit, sending shivers throughout my body.

"Oh baby, I'll fuck you when I'm ready. Right now, I want to redden your ass, so your pussy will have to wait," He whispers into my ear.

OH MY GOD...

I wake up drenched in sweat. The throbbing in my sex needs immediate release. I slide my hand into my panties, my finger gliding between my slick folds. I can't believe how wet I am...all from a dream. And what a dream is was! I remove my soaked finger and cover my clit with my juices. My dream replays in my head as I apply more pressure. My hips begin to grind into my hand, the glorious sensation building...my breathing becomes shallow as my release pulsates through my body.

Thankfully, it's Sunday and I could sleep in, after my middle of the night, one-woman rendezvous. My O relaxed me enough and I got a few more hours sleep. Brushing my teeth, I start thinking about last night...the flogging, the real one and the one in my dream. I turn, lifting my shirt and pulling my panties down, as I look in the mirror. No marks...no redness...no pink. Nothing to physically prove the pain and pleasure I experienced. I can't deny I'm a little disappointed.

I piddle around the house a bit and decide to lose myself in a book the rest of the day. My phone rings, pulling me from the world of fiction, I see Ben's picture on my screen.

"Hey mom, what cha up to today?"

"Hey hon! Nothing much, just taking it easy. How are you? How's school?"

Sundays are catch up days with the boys, if they don't come home for the weekend. Ben's finishing his junior year of college and Matt's finishing his first.

"I'm doing good. School is good, too. Um, speaking of school...I've got something to talk to you about."

"O-kay..." I reply cautiously.

"Don't worry...it's nothing bad," he chuckles into the phone. "My professor asked me if I would be interested in a scholarship to study abroad this summer. It's a six-week internship in France specializing in International Business."

"Oh my gosh Ben, that's awesome! What a great opportunity!" I squeal.

"The scholarship will cover most of the expenses, but there are some expenses that aren't. Room and board are covered with an allowance for food along with the classes, of course. I'm responsible for travel expenses, plus I need at least three suits with shirts and ties that are interchangeable, a passport, an international cell phone, and a voice activated translator would be helpful."

My mind is reeling trying to comprehend it all.

"Mom, I know this is a lot and I don't want to burden

you. I don't have to do this," he says sympathetically.

"Oh YES you do," I assert.

"I can try to get more hours at the grill to help cover some expenses," he offers.

"No...absolutely not. You work enough hours as it is and still keep your grades up. Don't worry, I'll figure something out. You just tell your professor that you're accepting the scholarship and I'll handle the rest," I assure him.

"Thanks, mom. You're the best!"

"Yeah, yeah..." I laugh. "I love you son and I'm so very proud of you!"

"I love you too, mom! Talk to you soon."

Now, what am I going to do? Tax season is over and so is the extra income. I could try to get a loan, but I know I can't get one at a decent rate and I don't really know exactly how much Ben's going to need. I need to process the information and think it through before I make any decisions.

Chapter 8

The morning is dragging by. As busy as I've been, surely it should be lunchtime. I grab my phone and shoot Deb a text.

Me: lunch???

Debra: Sure! I can get away around 1pm.

Me: 1pm ~ Delancy's

Debra: See ya then!

A later lunch is good...I should be able to finish this report before I go.

"Hey Sexy!" hisses in my ear.

I look up as Rick takes up residence on the corner of my desk. *Get your ass off my desk, slimeball.*

"How 'bout lunch, beautiful?" slithers from his lips.

Fuck NO!

"Sorry, Rick. I've already got plans for lunch."

He hears the same response every time he

asks. *Richard Foster, aka Rick, more like Dick - 100% sleaze. Married, but a huge flirt. Tries to cop a feel from any woman he can. Grabbed my ass once, and I threatened to break his wrist if it happened again. You would think he would get the message. He should have been reported by now, but he has 4 kids and his wife is nice and a little naïve. Losing his job would be devastating to his family.*

"How 'bout dessert?" He winks.

"How about you get your ass off my desk!!!" I snarl.

"Alright, alright...," he says, throwing up his hands in surrender and walking away.

Once he's out of sight, I grab my bag and head to the elevator.

"Jean, I'm heading to lunch with Debra. Want to join us?" I ask.

"Not today, Kathy. I had an appointment this morning, so I took an early lunch. Thanks for asking. I'll hold your calls for you," Jean replies cheerfully.

"Thanks! Be back in an hour."

****

"Hey Chicka?"

"Hey, Girlie..." I reply, folding my newspaper.

"Any luck?"

"No," I sigh, letting out a lung full of air. "It's been two weeks and not one prospect. Looking for a part-time job is sometimes harder than looking for one full-time. They're either the wrong hours and won't work with my current schedule or too far away to be worth the trip. I've got to get something lined up quick. Ben leaves for France the first of July."

"You'll find something, hon. Try not to worry," Deb reassures. "Do you have a backup plan?"

"Not one I want," I groan, opening my newspaper again.

"Hand me part of the paper and I'll help you search while we're waiting."

Handing her part of the paper, Deb starts batting her hand in the air...

"HEY, hey...," She whispers loudly. "Isn't that Master Patrick?"

"Where???" My eyes flitting all over the restaurant.

"Right there...in line," Deb replies in a panicked whisper.

"I don't see h-h...HOLY CRAP!" I dart my eyes away. "He saw me looking."

Waiting a minute or so, we both chance another look in his direction.... He WINKS!

"Oh, Shit...that's him!" I shrill, ducking our heads back in the newspaper.

Taking a deep breath to calm my nerves, I continue searching the paper as does Deb, even after they waiter brings our food. I circle a couple of prospects to check out. We've built a makeshift wall with the newspaper, to hide in our embarrassment, hoping he leaves soon.

His sultry, raspy voice pierces the silence, "Hello ladies."

Slowly, Deb and I bring down our paper fortress, and drink in tall, dark, and sexy. Seconds pass, which seem like an eternity. I'm waiting for Deb to say something first, but no... she's been stricken with the dumbfounded look again. The same one she was stricken with in Nexus, two weeks ago. The one my glare won't penetrate. *Damn her!*

I finally gather my wits, stammering my reply.

"Hi...M-m-m, Patrick." *Shit...what am I supposed to call him? Surely I don't call him Master in public.* "What brings you here?" I ask.

What do you think brought him here? It's a restaurant, dumbass.

"Delancy's makes the best Italian subs. When I'm in the neighborhood, I stop by," he explains.

"Yes, they have great subs and salads," I acknowledge.

"I hope you ladies enjoyed the open house," he continues, looking back and forth between us. Though it wasn't registering on Deb's face... *still dumbfounded.*

"Yes, we did. We had a wonderful time," I insist.

"Great! I look forward to seeing you both again real soon," he beams with a sexy smile.

I had no other response, but to smile and nod. Knowing I could never afford to go back. *Maybe the next open house. When it's free! Oh to see 'Adonis'...I mean Master Isaac again. To feel his hands on my skin. A shiver running down my spine.*

"If you have questions about anything, anything at all, feel free to call. The club offers orientation classes for beginners," he offers.

Again, I could only smile and nod.

"Thanks for the information. I'll keep that in mind." Finally finding my footing to make some semblance of a response.

"Well, it was nice seeing you, Katherine," reaching for my hand and bringing it to his lips. "And you as well, Debra," reaching for her hand and gently taking it, as she is still frozen and unable to move. He walks away leaving me with a gaping mouth and Deb, a statue.

"Wow...what a surprise to see him!" I muse.

"Yeah...a surprise," Deb murmurs still a little mesmerized.

"I can't believe he remembers our names."

"Me either,"

"Are you ready? I need to get back. I found a couple of prospects I want to call about."

“Yep, I need to get back, too. Do you see the waiter? He hasn’t brought us the bill,” Deb asks, scanning the crowded restaurant.

I wave down the waiter and he comes over.

“Hi... I know you’re busy, but can we get our bill? We need to get back to work,” I ask politely.

“I’m sorry you’ve been waiting, mam,” the waiter replies, looking a little confused. “Your bill’s been taken care of.”

“Taken care of...by who?” I inquire.

“The gentleman that you were speaking with. He took care of it,” he says walking away. Deb and I just stare at each other. *Dumbfounded...*

****

It’s been a really productive afternoon, plowing through the data Jean had for me when I returned from lunch. Definitely happy Jean wasn’t able to join us for lunch today. Our little visit with Patrick would’ve been awkward. Hell, it was awkward, but at least I didn’t have to explain him to Jean. She would have been all over that, trying to play matchmaker.

"Oooh, Kathy, he's a good looking man. He looks like a nice catch. Is he married? Dating?" Like he would be interested in me. I chuckle to myself. She's been trying to find me a man for years.

Gathering my things to leave for the day, I take a look at the employment ads I circled at lunch. The first one I called when I returned from lunch had already been filled. I read over the second ad again: *Part-time clerical help needed. Evening and weekend hours. Accounting knowledge a plus.*

I decide to call before I leave the office, in case they're closed when I get home.

"Thank you for calling J & J Contractors. How may I help you?" An elderly, yet firm female voice greets me.

"Good afternoon. My name is Katherine Stevens and I'm calling to inquire about the part-time clerical position that's available. The ad didn't list much information," I reply.

"Ah... yes, Ms. Stevens, I'll share the information I have. It's part-time, evening and weekend hours. The hours are somewhat flexible. More specific information can be obtained from the owner during an interview. Would you like me to schedule an interview for you?"

Pausing a brief second… "Yes, mam. That would be great."

"I know the owner's wanting to fill the position as soon as possible," she offers. "Can you meet this Wednesday? He's available at five or six pm."

"Six would be perfect."

"Great, I'll pencil you in for Wednesday at 6pm. If you have any questions, please give me a call, my name is Ms. Glancey."

"Thank you, Ms. Glancey. I look forward to seeing you on Wednesday."

****

Isaac

"What's up, Ike? I saw your truck outside, so I thought I'd stop by. What the hell are you doing here so late?" Patrick announces as he walks through the door.

"I'm trying to get these damn books caught up for the club," I growl, running my hands across my eyes. "It's been a busy week here and I had to go to Greenville for two days to bid a job, so the books got behind...again," I grumble. "What are you doing out this late riding around?"

"Working a case, man...working a case," Patrick chuckles. "So I take it you've had no luck finding someone to help out at Nexus."

"Man, I've interviewed twelve people in the past two weeks, and still no luck. This is going to be harder than I originally thought. You just can't advertise... *hey you want to work in a BDSM club.* Edna left me a message that I have another interview Wednesday. It would be a helluva lot easier if I could find somebody at the club."

"Oh, by the way, I saw the redhead and her friend from the open house, today at Delancey's. I asked them about their open house experience and welcomed them back. They said, well Red said, they had a great time. I think her friend's a little shy," Patrick chuckles again.

Obviously remembering something, I'm not privy to.

"I also mentioned the newbie orientation that's offered at the club," he rambles on.

"Really..." I ponder. *Damn, I'd like to get hold of that ass again. Light it up and shove my cock deep in that pussy. Shit... just the thought and I'm rock hard.* "Delancey's, huh?"

"Yeah...I picked up their check. You know, customer relations and all," Patrick beams with that shit eatin' grin of his.

"Hell, man. Let's get out of here and grab a beer.

****

Damn, Rick needs to hurry up and bring me the Syntec portfolio. It's four o'clock and I need to get that report finished today. I don't want to be late for my interview at six and traffic will be a nightmare.

"Here ya go gorgeous." *FINALLY, ... slow ass.* "Thanks Rick," I say, trying to be cordial.

"So what do you say we grab a drink after work?" He schmoozes, sitting his ass on my desk...AGAIN.

"Seriously, do you mind not sitting on my desk?" I snap, rolling my eyes. "And NO...no drink for me.
Sorry..." *Sorry...NOT!*

"Come on, babe..."

"BABE! Don't call me that...I'm not your, BABE!" I snarl. *Grrrr... stupid prick.*

"Just a term of endearment, Kathy."

"Spare me your endearments. Share them with your wife." I scold. *For God's sake...GO AWAY so I can work!* "Seriously, Rick...I need to get this report finished."

Taking the hint from the sledgehammer over the head, he walks away.

****

Report finished, I head to the restroom to check my hair and make-up. Damn, it's almost five thirty... I gotta go. I grab my things and nearly sprint to my car. Well, I sprint as much as my fat ass will let me.

As I expected, I hit a wall of traffic. I'm cutting this very close. *Please don't let me be late...I hate being late.* With five minutes to spare, I pull into the parking lot of J & J Contractors.

I step into the reception area. It's very quiet...too quiet. *Where is everyone? Today is Wednesday, right?* What I assume is the secretary's desk, looks tidied up for the day, several stacks of folders and invoices, neatly stacked. Chair neatly pushed in.... Ms. Glancey's desk and she appears to be gone for the day.

"Hello," I quietly call out. Not sure if I really want anyone to answer. "Hello...is anyone here?" I call a little louder.

"Sorry to keep you waiting...," a voice coming from the other room, echoing, like it's inside a tunnel. "I just got back from a job and I need to clean up a bit. My secretary leaves at five. I tried to get back in time to get cleaned up before you got here, but we had a problem that kept me longer," the voice continues, still somewhat distorted.

"No problem...take your time," I call back to the voice. "I had an issue at work that delayed me, as well. I was worried I would be late for the interview," I chime back.

"Seems like it's been an afternoon full of problems," the voice sounds again, a little closer and clearer. "I haven't even had a chance to read my secretary's notes to find out your name," the sultry sound even closer, coming toward where I'm standing.

My gaze set firmly in the direction of the voice, to see the person the voice emanates from. "My name is Katherine ...OH, MY GOD!"

Chapter 9

"Katherine Ohmygod...interesting name," a chuckle escapes his lips. "Isaac Jameson," he says extending his hand to me.

I can't move, can't speak. *What do I say? Oh, hey there, stranger that I let spank my ass two weeks ago.* His hand is hanging in midair, as his eyes search my face, my eyes. I want to look away, but I can't. I want to turn and run, but I can't. My heart is pounding in my chest.

"W-W-what are you doing here?" I utter with the breath I've been holding.

"Well, this is my company and it seems that I'm about to interview you for a job," he says matter-of-factly.

"No...no...no," I breathlessly whisper. "I-I can't." My eyes still not able to tear away from his.

He steps closer, a look of concern on his face, gently taking both my hands.

"Are you okay, Katherine? Here, come have a seat in my

office." The heat from his body melts the ice that has me frozen still, leading me into the room he just emerged from.

Sitting in the chair across from his desk, I take a deep, calming breath. "I'm fine. Really...I am. Just a little shocked," I insist. He hands me a bottle of water and I thank him, as he takes a seat behind his desk.

"Well, I don't want to waste your time and I feel fine, so I'll see my way out."

"See your way out? Aren't you here to interview for a job?"

Bringing my eyes back to his gorgeous face, "Um, well...I don't think that would be appropriate, considering what I allowed you – a perfect stranger, to do to me. Do you? I'm sure your opinion of me is not very high."

"First of all, you have no idea what my opinion is of you. Second, I happened to enjoy flogging your ass. Third, don't EVER speak negatively about yourself, especially in front of me. I don't like it," he growls, a fierce look in his eyes, looking deep into mine.

A shiver streaks through my body, "Yes, Sir."

Pushing himself back in his chair, a calmness on his

face, “Now, you’re obviously interested in a part-time job, so I’m assuming you have one full-time.”

“Yes, Sir.” *Again with the Sir... get a grip, girl.*

“May I ask why you’re interested in a part-time job?”

Wringing my hands in my lap...I’m so nervous. I take another deep breath.

“My oldest son won a scholarship for a six week internship to France to study International Business. There are incidental expenses not covered. I want to help him all I can,” I explain.

Silence lingers as Isaac relaxes back in his chair, fingers linked together, resting behind his head; his gaze fixated on me. I shift uncomfortably in my chair, eyes shifting across the floor, quickly peering up to catch his expression, as I clear my throat.

“I hope your son realizes how lucky he is to have a mom like you.”

“I have two sons. I do what I can to help them.”

“Husband or significant other?” He asks, with a slight bite in his tone.

"Of course NOT!" I shriek. "Do you think I would let you spank me and rub your hands all over my ass, if I was married or attached in any way?!?!" I storm. *I know this is an interview of sorts...but does he think I'm a whore??? He spanked my ass and I didn't know him...so whore is a possibility.*

"I'm just clarifying before we proceed any further discussing the job. And I'm ignoring your sassy mouth, for the moment, but I won't continue ignoring it," he says with a hint of threat behind the words.

Sassy mouth...me??? And what does having a husband have to do with the job?

"As the ad stated, I'm looking for someone with good clerical skills to work nights and weekends. Accounting skills would be perfect. I assume you have these skills?"

"I'm an accountant for a PR firm, so yes, I have the skills you're looking for," I reply.

"Do you run a second shift here, or would it be just me in the office at night and on the weekends?"

"Well, you see...the job is not for the construction company. The job is at Nexus."

"Nexus? I don't understand. The ad said the job was here, well...I mean...I assumed since the interview was here, the job was here. Ms. Glancey said that I needed to get more information from the owner. I show up here and you're here. Are you the owner of this business? I'm sorry, I'm a little confused," I babble on.

"Yes, I own J & J Contractors. I own Nexus, too," he reveals. I sit with my mouth gaped open, trying to gather my thoughts. I'm sure it's a similar look to Deb's dumbfounded look at Patrick. I'm a little taken aback.

"I can't very well advertise a job in a BDSM club. I have to be discreet. I broach the subject very carefully. I interview first to get an idea, then call them back for a second interview if I think there's potential. No need with you, you are quite familiar with the club," he says with a wicked smile. "So are you still interested?"

"Go on...," I reply skeptically.

"I need someone to help keep the office organized and the books caught up. We're open four nights a week, Wednesday through Saturday. You wouldn't have to work all four nights, but at least three. It's not hard, just time consuming. Edna, Ms. Glancey was handling the books until about six months ago."

"Does she know what goes on at Nexus?" I interrupt.

"She has an idea," he chuckles, breaking into a big smile.

Mmm... dimples.

"Sorry...for interrupting. Please continue."

"As I was saying, Edna had a heart attack six months ago. She's stubborn and wouldn't retire, but I wouldn't allow her to continue with the added work of the club. I've been trying to keep up with it, but it's proving to be a little too much with everything I have to do here."

Isaac was talking to me, but it felt like he was admitting it to himself.

"Your employment will include membership to the club and its facilities. When your shift is over, you are free to enjoy the club," he offers.

"Oh, no problem. I have no plans to participate at the club, Sir...I mean Mr. Jameson." *I need to lay the boundaries now. Strictly professional...Mr. Jameson, Mr. Jameson, Mr. Jameson.*

"Isaac, please...Mr. Jameson was my dad, and all employees participate at the club. No voyeurs at the club, except visitors at open house, and that includes staff. I want members to feel at ease, not like they're on display. We have some very prominent members from Atlanta and the surrounding areas; CEOs, political figures, sports figures, and entertainers. They come to Nexus, because unlike the larger clubs downtown, we are smaller and cater to their need for privacy."

Isaac's demeanor is all business as he justifies this expectation.

I shudder to ask this, "What about dress code? Do you have one?"

Isaac rests his elbows on his desk, steepling his index fingers at his lips, those thick, suckable lips. His chestnut eyes smoldering into mine, igniting a fire between my thighs.

"The purple corset is perfect," a devilish smile emerging on his face.

"You mean I have to wear sexy clothes?" *Dumb question...It's a BDSM club. You can't stroll up in khakis and a cardigan.*

"Yes, Katherine...sexy clothes, as you put it. Again, making our members feel comfortable," he reiterates. "Is that a problem?" He asks raising an eyebrow.

"It's just that, well...I don't look..."

"Stop, right there!" He demands. "I believe I made myself clear when I said not to make negative comments about yourself."

"Yes, but I don't want to be an embarrassment to your business. They want to see beautiful, skinny women."

"Katherine...Stop. Now." He utters in a voice so low and menacing, I'd rather him yell. "Not another word," he fumes.

I have to say this is the most intense interview I've ever had. The lines we've crossed and the sexual tension I feel is consuming me. I should be running out the door. But I'm drawn like a moth to the flame. I feel so alive around him, energized, thrilled. Isaac Jameson does something to me I don't recognize in myself.

"So Katherine...will you take the job?"

"Yes..."

****

Isaac

What the hell am I gonna do now? I've got to get my head straight. Do I really want her working at the club?

Maybe I should rethink this. She knows very little of the lifestyle, but I think she would be great organizing the paper work and keeping the books straight at Nexus. She really doesn't need to know much about the lifestyle. I can teach her what she needs to know. *My cock stirs awake at that thought.*

Shit, I can't teach her. I don't play with staff. *Damn...* I could get Patrick or Derek or one of the other Doms to get her more familiar with it. That would be best. I don't like the feeling I have when she's around. Possessive...very possessive. I feel it tugging at me, urging me to lock her away and keep her all to myself.

Her lush ass and beautiful tits...MINE. No, not yours. I felt it immediately...the first time I laid eyes on her. *Those fucking gorgeous eyes, I want to drown in them.*

I've never had this possessive feeling for any woman, not even my ex-wife. *Obviously my conscientious knew what a cheating bitch she was.* And I damn sure wasn't possessive of Vickie and she was my sub for Christ sake. *Well, supposed to be my sub, but conniving whore and undermining wench don't exactly fall into the submissive category.* Exactly why the rules about playing with the staff are in place.

Yes, Patrick and Derek can familiarize Katherine with the activities in the club. I will keep a safe distance. They will make sure she's protected. *No...that's my job, my ass, my tits. No, no, no...shit!*

Maybe she really doesn't need familiarizing. She'll be really busy with the paperwork and accounting. I need to rethink her job description. Yeah, that's just what I'll do.

Chapter 10

Wrapping up my workday, I chuckle to myself, recalling the conversation with Deb explaining my new job.

"You took a job where?" Deb shrieked through the phone.

"Nexus." I reply. Still not believing it myself.

"I don't understand. I thought your interview was at some construction company," She states questioningly.

"It was...at J & J Contractors, but the job is actually at Nexus."

"Doing what...getting your ass flogged?" Her belly laugh roaring through the phone.

"Hardy, har, har... you so funny," I quip. "I'll be organizing and taking care of the books."

"I'm still confused. Why did you go to the construction company?"

"Well, the owner of the construction company owns

Nexus, too." I explain.

"Oh…wow!"

"Ha, you don't know the 'WOW', yet," I tease.

"Huh???"

"I mean the surprising part is 'WHO' owns Nexus; the person I'll be working for. You'll never guess."

"Who?" She demands.

"Isaac…Master Isaac," I exclaim.

"Uh-uh…no way! Are you SERIOUS???"

Isaac and I agreed that I would start this Friday night, so I make my way to the lingerie store. I want to blend in tomorrow night when I start my new job.

Much quicker than the last time, I have my outfit selected; a black corset dress with off-the shoulder cuff sleeves. The sleeves cover the swaying part of my arm, the corset cinches my fluffy midsection, and the dress part falls mid-thigh; sexy but not too revealing and it's on clearance. Perfect!

****

Taking a deep breath, I step out of my car and make my way to the entrance of the club. It's still a few hours before the club opens, but Isaac wants to go over the accounting software and procedures before it gets busy.

Opening the door, I proceed over to the check in counter.

"Come on back..." his gruff voice calls out. *Isaac. No, I'm in the club. He's Master Isaac...*

I slothfully make my way around the counter toward his voice. I step into the door way. Master Isaac is sitting behind his desk, with a phone up to his ear, talking about measurements of something and clearly absorbed in paperwork on his desk. He motions with his hand for me to come on in. I take a couple more steps forward, but feeling like I'm invading his privacy, I stop and begin looking around the walls for something to distract me. A set of time-lapsed photos of a building under construction catches my attention, so I step over to have a closer look. My eyes continue to peruse the office. I notice a triangular shaped case with an American flag inside sitting on a small bookcase. I saunter over to have a closer look. Beside the flag, slightly out of view, is a framed accommodation from the U.S. Navy Construction Training Center, *presented to Isaac Jameson – Seabees - "We Build, We Fight"*, embossed on the certificate.

A guttural growl draws my attention back to Isaac.

"You look beautiful, Katherine." My breath catches in my throat as his smoldering gaze envelops me. Just as quickly, his face subtly changes and a more controlled look emerges. "Thank you, Sir."

"How long were you in the Navy?" I inquire nosily. *It's really none of my business and he may get offended I asked. Oh, well...too late now.*

"Twenty years."

He doesn't look old enough to have spent twenty years in the Navy. The look of dismay on my face solicits more information from him.

"I enlisted when I was eighteen, retired at thirty-eight. I took over the construction company from my dad when I retired, a little over ten years ago."

"Are you married?" I ask, pushing my luck.

"Of course not. Would I have spanked and had my

hands all over your bare ass, if I was?" He fed my words back to me.

"Touché, Mr. Jameson."

He moves another chair behind his desk. "Have a seat and let's get started." He pats the seat beside him.

"Here are my medical records," I offer, handing him my records.

He peruses through the paperwork, appearing to mentally note what was pertinent to him.

"Birth control is blank."

"Sorry...tubal ligation after my second child. It's been so long I forget to list it," I stammer.

"I'll make note of that on the form."

As I sit down in this straight back chair, I notice how my large breast are now pushed up under my chin. Dear lord, they're about to plop out on his desk. I'm silently willing them to stay put.

God...he smells delicious. I'm trying to pay attention to what he's saying. Thankfully, it's a basic accounting system that I'm very familiar with, otherwise I'd be lost. He suddenly reaches across me to get a binder, his forearm brushes across my left breast, sending a bolt of energy to my sex. Oh my god, I'm too close to him. I want to nuzzle in the crevice of his neck, inhaling his scent, running my tongue along the trail. *Pull yourself together girl.*

"Any questions?" He asks, drawing me from my naughty thoughts.

"No...I think I'm good for now," hoping he didn't notice my zoning out.

"Gina will be checking people in tonight. She will show you that aspect of it. Signing members in is all Gina's trained to do. She monitors the door in lieu of paying membership dues. One of the Dungeon Monitors covers the door when she's not here or during her play time. You can join in that rotation, too, but only if the paperwork is caught up. That's more important than Gina scening," he chides.

I sense that's a touchy issue.

"Unfortunately, there's a lot of paperwork to catch up, but don't feel you have to finish it all tonight. Make time to check out the club."

"No worries about that, Sir. I'd rather get the work caught up. I'm not in a hurry to get out in the club, just yet," I offer.

"Oh, Katherine...have your forgotten? No voyeurs...you must participate," he asserts. "However, in the beginning I'd rather you observe different scenes to familiarize yourself and get more comfortable. For the foreseeable future, I only want you scening with Club Masters; Master Derek, Master Patrick, and of course, myself. You can identify Club Masters by the black armband on their arm. Club Masters have been through extensive training in the lifestyle and safety," he implores.

Reaching into his desk drawer, he pulls out a strip of leather. I follow his lead and stand, though I'm sure my legs are shakier than his.

"Hold your hair up and turn around," he commands, placing the leather around my neck. "This is the club collar," he explains. "It signifies that you're under the protection of the club, of me. No Dom is allowed to scene with you without my permission. It doesn't mean you're my sub, it means you have my protection. Do you understand?"

I can't deny that a pang of hurt just seared through my heart at his statement, *'you're not my sub'. Of course I'm not. Good grief girl, get a grip.*

"Yes Sir. I understand."

Besides, no one's going to ask to scene with me. I don't think I need the collar, I think to myself as I stroke my finger across it, tracing the letters *N-E-X-U-S*.

"If you have any questions or problems with the paperwork or accounting, find me. I'm the only one who handles that...well, until now," he explains.

"I understand, Sir."

"Panties, Katherine? Are you wearing panties?" He asks with an emblazoned glare.

Shocked by his question, it took me a moment to respond. Finally, I answer in a breathless whisper..., "Yes".

Dropping to his knee, instantly Isaac's hand is under my dress pulling my panties to the floor. Frozen in place, without prompting, I step out of them. He quickly stands bringing them to his face, inhaling deeply.

"You smell so fucking good," he growls.

Tucking my panties in his pocket, he turns and walks out of the office.

****

Isaac

Looking up, I catch my first glance at her...black corset dress. Those tits rounding out of the top. Damn, I want to clench those hard nubs between my teeth. The growl that escaped my chest caught her attention. Her gaze meets mine...those beautiful eyes. The things I want to do to her, while I look into those eyes. God, she's fucking beautiful.

I motion for her to sit next to me. I explain the software, but her tits are about to tumble onto my desk. *I want her bent over my desk, tits spilling out, my hands on her bare ass, while I bury my cock in her pussy. Fuck man, pay attention...*

I finally end the rambling about the paperwork. I explain her rules for playing. I hadn't planned on putting the club collar on her, but the urge is overwhelming. I don't want every fucking guy in here thinking he's gonna get a 'go' with her. HELL NO!

I place the club collar around her neck. I should place MY collar on her. *No...not going there again. Get your head on straight. Keep your distance.*

I see her briefly clench her jaw when I explain what the collar means. I need to remember this is all new for her. *But I do love keeping her on edge.*

Just as I suspected, she's wearing panties. I don't want her wearing panties, although I haven't told her as much. *Yeah, I want them off...* I want the smell of her bare pussy on my chair.

Fuck...she smells so fucking good. I want to run my tongue between her fat lips, locking her pink pearl between my teeth. I want her taste on my tongue. *Fuck, fuck, fuck...*

Mmm...black lace and her scent. They're mine now... *Damn, I'm gonna owe her a fortune in panties.*

****

After gathering my chin off the floor, while Isaac leaves with my panties, *that's the second pair he's taken,* I get busy familiarizing myself with the paperwork.

"Well, hey there." This chirpy voice startles me. "I didn't mean to scare you. I stood here a few seconds, but you seem pretty focused on what you're working on," the chirpy voice continues.

Chirpy voice belonged to 'Blond bombshell', which I now know is Gina.

"Hi, I'm Kathy. You must be Gina," I say getting up to shake her hand.

"That's me." Gina responds. "Hey, I remember you from the open house," she gasps. I nod in acknowledgement.

"Master Isaac told me last night that he hired someone. I'm supposed to show you how to sign in members. It's pretty simple," she explains.

I decide this would be a good time to give my eyes a rest from the computer screen, so I head to the check in desk to get schooled in membership sign in.

Gina's very talkative and animated. She's very sweet. She also seems to be in the know about what goes on in the club. Who's with who, who's single, and who to steer clear of.

My ears really perk up when she begins talking about Master Isaac's former sub.

"Vickie was a real piece of work. I was lucky that she left shortly after I started coming here over a year ago," Gina cautions.

"Why did she leave?" I ask, not able to keep my curiosity to myself. I really shouldn't be nosing in his business.

Gina began looking around before whispering, "She's a manipulative bitch. She would do stupid crap and then blame others, especially unattached subs; threatening to have Master Isaac kick us out. We were scared to say anything to Master Isaac because after all, she was his sub. Thankfully, some of the other Masters found out about her conniving ways and made Master Isaac aware. He uncollared her and she left. Master Isaac hasn't taken a sub since. He helps train them and plays...that's it," she confides, as she continues scoping the area for eavesdroppers.

I ponder the information that Gina shared, while I continue working. The thoughts of Isaac having a sub or playing with others, really pisses me off. I know I have no right to have these feelings, but I can't help the way I feel.

"Well, hello Katherine," the sultry voice announced. I'm so lost in my thoughts and work, that I didn't notice Patrick standing at the door.

"Hi," I reply.

"Master Isaac says it's time for you to wrap up the work and come out to play."

Chapter 11

"I have a demo in a bit, so I'm gonna make my rounds checking on activities and scenes. You can join me and observe the different types of play," Patrick offers as I tidy up the desk.

"Thank you, Master Patrick. That would be great," I lie in response. *I just want to stay hidden in this office. I'm not sure my psyche can handle the play that goes on here.*

I follow Master Patrick to different scenes. Most are tolerable, not causing me to gasp or make a fool of myself. We walk up behind a small gathering of people watching a scene. I realize it's Mistress Charlotte and her sub, Edward. Deb and I met them at Open House. *Edward's caged cock instantly appears in my head.*

Edward's delicious body is lying on what looks like an inversion table, that's inclined at a forty-five-degree angle. His hands and ankles are bound and he is spread eagle at the mercy of his Mistress. Red wax drips from the candle in Charlotte's hand, trailing it down his rippled abs. A swishing gasp of air escapes from Edwards lips with each searing drop.

The wax is inching closer to Edward's thick erect cock. I quickly turn my back, not wanting to witness what I'm certain is about to happen. Sensing my apprehension, Master Patrick takes my elbow and we begin to walk away. Within moments, a blood curdling growl erupts. A shiver rips through me, knowing the wax arrived at its intended destination.

Master Patrick leads me over to another small gathering of people. "It's time for my demonstration. Care to hang out and watch?"

"That would be great," I reply. "Are you demonstrating the flogger again, like you did at Open House?"

"No, a mini bull whip... basic strokes and such."

"O-oh...," I stammer, trying to appear nonchalant. *HOLY CRAP...a freakin' whip!!!*

Master Patrick gently guides me to the front of the small crowd, giving me a better view. *Probably to make me more uncomfortable.*

Master Derek saunters up beside me. We haven't officially met, but I definitely remember his caramel dipped, muscular body from Open House and Deb's bondage scene with him.

“Hey Katherine...I’m Master Derek,” he introduces himself, his ebony eyes pinning me.

Damn, do I have a flashing sign above my head? *Katherine...the new kid in town.*

“Nice to meet you, Master Derek,” I reply shaking his offered hand.

We stand watching Patrick crack the whip from side to side, as he explains the appropriate techniques. I’m intrigued with the deadly snap of the whip, yet it leaves barely a mark on the woman attached to the cross. Just then, Patrick calls my name and motions for me to join him. *SHIT...SHIT...SHIT!!!* He calls my name again with an expectant look in his eyes. The urge to bolt and run nearly overcomes me. The pressing need to keep this job surges forward in my thoughts, trumping my fears. I reluctantly make my way to his side.

“Alright, Katherine...lets you and I have a go at this. What do you say?” His suggestion laced with a hint of demand. My stomach immediately goes to my throat.

“I don’t think I’m ready for this, Sir,” I whisper my concern.

“You’ll be fine, Katherine. I promise. I’m just going to give you a few samples of different strokes. You need to experience this with me, so you have an idea before you decide to scene with someone else."

Quickly, I'm bound to the cross and Master Patrick delivers a sampling of his forte. I can't believe when the first couple of strikes barely graze my skin, like a tickling stroke. The intensity gradually increases, with the last strike feeling like someone quickly touching my back with a sparkler; quickly searing, then dissipating. Patrick quickly comes over to check on me and then releases my restraints.

"How was it?"

"The beginning was great, very relaxing. However, I'm not so sure I'll be standing in line to experience this much," I reply with a half-hearted laugh.

Master Patrick continues discussing his demonstration with the onlookers. My throat is very dry, so I head to the bar for a bottle of water. Water in hand, I'm people watching as Master Isaac approaches.

"So how big of a mess is it?" Master Isaac inquires.

Mesmerized by his close proximity, it takes a minute for his inquiry to register in my brain. *Well...it's a brain until he comes around, then it's mush.*

"It's not that bad." I chuckle, trying to gain and keep my composure. "I've been checking out different scenes tonight, like you asked me to." I offer.

"Good girl."

How can two words make my panties wet and my sex throb?

"We'll continue some training now. Follow me," Master Isaac motions, as he walks toward the lounge area. He sinks into an oversized, cushiony chair. I stand there not sure what to do.

"Have a seat on the pillow," he nods to the pillow beside his chair.

"Many Doms like their subs to sit at their feet, near them. This allows closeness to their sub; for stroking and petting. Personally, I like it sometimes and sometimes I want you in my lap, or in a chair beside me. I will make my desire known at the time, as most Doms will let their sub know. Communication is key. If your Dom doesn't communicate, that's a red flag for you," he explains stroking my right breast that he's removed from my corset. That I allowed him to remove without any hesitancy. *What the hell is wrong with me?* I nod my acknowledgement.

"I welcome your conversation Katherine. Some Doms want their subs to remain quiet unless a direct question is asked. Again, I will communicate to you if I wish you to remain silent. I believe you to have good social manners, and that will be the norm unless otherwise directed."

I release a soft gasp of air as he rolls my nipple between his thumb and index finger, pinching the hard nub periodically.

He releases my nipple and gathers a handful of my hair, firmly but gently, guiding me to stand, then leading me to his lap. I'm shocked at his forwardness, yet I offer no resistance. My body becomes rigid with the thought of how wanton I must appear to the audience sitting around us.

I soften into Isaac as he begins seducing my nipple with his tongue; wickedly flicking it like the forked-tongue of a serpent. His lips envelope my breast, continuing to lavish my nipple. Pain intrudes as his teeth grip the elongated nub, sucking further into his mouth; simultaneously, he pinches my other nipple. Just as quick, he releases his savage hold and caresses the pain away with the softness of his lips. He repeats this diabolical process over and over. I'm squirming fitfully on his hard cock, that's resting at the crack of my ass.

"I smell your arousal," he growls in my ear, as he nips

the lobe. "Don't come until I say to," he demands.

A shudder erupts through my body. He releases my breast and moves his free hand under my dress and explores between my sodden folds with his finger.

"You're so wet for me, baby."

I know I should be ashamed, feel some sort of indignity...but I don't. I want him to fuck me. Here, there...wherever. His thumb gravitates to my clit; circling and teasing. My God...it's been so long since I felt this way. *Have I ever felt this? I don't think so.*

I'm grinding on his hardened shaft, at the same time grinding into his hand. The roughness of the denim material adding to my pleasure. I'm literally dry fucking him like a slut. *A very horny slut!*

"I think a naughty girl wants to be fucked," he groans.

"OH GOD YES, PLEASE...please!!!" I plead breathlessly.

"Please what...," he implores.

"Please, I need to come, Sir. Please...," I pant.

Isaac thrusts his finger into my drenched sex.

"You're so fucking wet. I want to sink my cock, balls deep in that wet pussy." He drags his sex coated finger through his lips. "You taste fucking amazing... like sweet peach nectar."

That is nearly my undoing...but NO! Isaac inserts a second finger thrusting in and out, unrelenting as his thumb applies more pressure to my clit. Assaulting my nipple again, the multiple sensations overwhelm me. The pressure in my sex is teetering on the brink of combustion.

"Come, NOW!" He growls.

My world is a haze as he pinches my clit sending violent shudders through my body. *AAAhhh.... I'm soaring!*

Unaware of the time that's passed, I slowly regain my composure. I've never experienced such a powerful orgasm; and from finger fucking.

Master Isaac cuddles me and nibbles my lower lip. Drawing me closer and deepening his kiss, I inhale a ragged breath, wincing in pain.

"What's wrong?" He coaxes as he sits me up, turning me to examine my body. He softly traces the welts from the whip.

"WHAT THE FUCK?!?!?"

Grabbing my arm, he quickly stands with me, my legs falling aimlessly to the floor. My heart is pounding and my mind racing. *Why's he so angry? What did I do???*

"Who the FUCK did this? He thunders. His eyes, cold and menacing. "No one fucking asked me to scene with you? You cannot scene with ANYONE without my permission." Isaac growls through clenched teeth. "I think I made myself very clear about that, Katherine. That's what the fucking collar is for!"

Trembling from his rant, his hand still firmly gripping my arm, I can't do anything but stare wide-eyed into his glare, mouth gaping. He takes my chin, drawing our faces closer together. I shiver...

"Answer me...," He demands in a frightening whisper.

"I...I..."

"Chill man...I did it," Patrick interrupts, placing a hand on Isaac's shoulder, then steps around to my side, facing Isaac. I didn't think Isaac's eyes could get more frightening, but they became deadly. Isaac broke his intense gaze on me and locked a lethal stare on Patrick.

"What did you say?" Isaac snaps at Patrick. *Oh lord, what have I done? Isaac is furious.*

"Calm down, Ike," Patrick let out a small chuckle. *What the hell is he laughing at? Is he crazy?* I think to myself.

"I didn't play with her. I gave her a few strikes in varying degrees, as part of my demonstration tonight. Just a sample for her, that's all," Patrick explains casually.

His explanation seems to have a calming effect as Master Isaac's look softens, somewhat, but not completely.

"I thought you wanted the Masters to give her an overview of the club, Ike. I'm sorry if I misunderstood."

"I did...I do. It was just unexpected," Isaac answers, though he still seems upset. "I didn't realize you would demo on her tonight. I'll clarify my expectations more clearly in the future," he grouses.

I'm swaying side to side, as I shift back and forth between my feet. It feels awkward listening to Patrick and Isaac talk about me, like I'm not standing here. I want to go back in the office. This is too much.

"Katherine, I'll meet you in my office shortly," Isaac

says, as if reading my mind. *Thank you, Jesus.*

****

Isaac

FUUUCK!!! I need to get a grip. She's not my sub... not mine. But god she felt so good in my arms. Her soft body nuzzled up to me. Her pussy so wet and I barely did anything. Why do I feel so tense, like ripping somebody apart? I don't want anybody touching her. I shouldn't feel like this. FUCK, FUCK, FUCK!

"Man you're sending mixed signals," Patrick accuses.

"What the hell are you talking about? To who?" I snarl back.

"To us...to her...to yourself."

"Psshh... keep your psychobabble to yourself, Pat. It's not a mixed signal, but your interpretation. I told you to help familiarize her with the club, not stripe her up."

"Why can't you just admit you're attracted to her, Ike? It's not the end of the world. You've never had an issue with us demoing on a sub, including yours. I demoed on Vickie, plenty of times, at your encouragement I might add and you never had a problem with it. Now, with Katherine, you want to rip somebody's head off. Man, she's a fine piece of ass. If you don't tap it, somebody will," Pat smirks as he walks off.

I'm gonna rip his fucking head off.

Shaking my head, trying to clear out the bullshit Pat's spewing, not wanting to listen to it anymore. *It'll never work, I'm not good for her.*

He's right about a mixed signal, but the only signal mixed is the one between my dick and my brain.

Chapter 12

The lobby is dim when I approach it. It's already closing time? The night has flown by. I head into the office to close out the books for the night; something that hasn't been done consistently, which screws up the daily logs.

The think-less task leaves my mind to wonder back to my horny escapade with Isaac. God, what was I thinking? I lose all my mental capacity when I'm around him. I allowed him to bring me to an orgasm, a man I barely know, and he did it with people watching. He must think I'm a slut. *Hell, I think I'm a slut.*

I feel a presence, gasping as I look up to see Master Isaac looming behind me.

"Hi...I was just closing out the books for the night. I noticed this is not being done every business day and it's really important that it gets done; to keep the accounting in order," I ramble on.

He doesn't make a sound...his gaze burning my skin. I stand, to put some distance between us and possibly get some air in my lungs, as he's taken my breath away.

Dumb move...now I'm trapped between the desk and his hulking body.

He glides his fingers gently through my hair, entwining them and tugging my face to meet his gaze.

"I...um, I don't know what came over me out there. I've never done that before," I whisper. "You have to believe..."

His mouth inhales my words as his tongue delves between my lips, exploring my mouth thoroughly. Hardening his kiss, I feel he's going to devour my soul. I match his exploration with heated fervor, running my fingers through his hair. He softens the kiss as he frames my face with his hands. Slowly he pulls away, quickly returning for another taste before nipping my swollen lip.

"Let me show you around the areas of the club off limits to members," He breathes onto my lips.

Quickly taking my hand, he leads me through the club and pass the bar area. I notice the club appears to be empty and dimly lit. My heart begins to race with a blend of anticipation and trepidation. Without a spoken word, he continues leading us down a hallway. Though it appears identical to the hallway where the theme rooms are located, this hallway looks desolate by comparison, with few doors, all unmarked.

We stop at the end of the hall, in front of an industrial type door with a keypad beside it. Remaining silent, Isaac stands beside me though he seems a million miles away. I believe the sound of my pounding heart brings his thoughts back to the here and now. He leans down, tucking a strand of my hair behind my ear, then placing a soft, chaste kiss on my lips.

He enters a number on the keypad then takes a key from his pocket to unlock the lock on the door. I pause for just a moment, unsure of where I'm going and quickly try to consider the level of my safety. The recondite area only heightens my anxiety. Isaac gently nudges me through the door and turns to lock it again.

Mahogany colored wooden walls, encase the stairs in front of me. Faux candle sconces discreetly light the staircase as we ascend to the second floor. At the top of the stairs, is a replica of the industrial door located at the bottom. Isaac repeats the process of entering a code in the keypad and unlocking the door. I step through the doorway, and literally into another world.

"Make yourself at home. Can I get you something to drink? Beer, wine, water?" He asks as he flips a switch on the wall, illuminating a modern contemporary living room.

"I'm fine. Thank you. Is this where you live?" I inquire as I pivot around slowly, taking in the view. It's warm and cozy, yet has a very modern feel. Definitely unlike any bachelor pad I've ever seen. I'm impressed.

I feel his eyes on me and mine find his. I get so lost in his eyes. He stares into my soul for a long moment, before answering. As if he's unsure he even wants to answer.

"Yes...," he answers has he softly kisses my lips. "I love the club, but I love my privacy more. This is my safe haven, my sanctuary," scorching my lips with his once again.

"I've never brought a woman up here."

His admission stuns me. His decision to bring me here, stuns me even more. *I wonder why he's never brought a woman here.*

"I've always used the club facilities for any play. The club has everything I need, no reason to bring them up here," he says, like he read my mind. *He does that a little too much for my comfort.* This information only baffles me more. *Why me? Why now?*

My thoughts scatter when he grabs a hand full of my

hair, tilting my face to his. He seizes my mouth savagely, my body instantly tensing in protest, then just as quickly molding into his form. He trails his lips along my jaw, down to my ear.

"I want to fuck you Katherine, but first I'm going to redden your ass," he groans, pinning me to the wall. "Can you think of a reason that I shouldn't?" He goads, as his fingers easily glide between my wet folds.

I'm trying to muster a response but I can't.

"Mmmm...this pussy is so wet, I think I know your answer, baby. But I need to hear it...now."

"Yes...I mean, no. I mean...I...please fuck me," I mutter.

"Say again," he demands, his darkened eyes penetrating my own.

"Sir, please fuck me, Sir," I pant so flustered I can't think straight.

"That's my good girl." Taking my hand, he leads me down the hall.

Once in his bedroom, he steps behind me, loosening my corset.

"Take it off...I want to see you."

My body freezes at his request. *I can't take my clothes off. No way!* I just stand here, frozen. This is going to end right now. He's a Dom, expecting submission. The thought of submitting to Isaac is thrilling, but I can't shed my clothes and stand nude in front of this beautiful man.

"Katherine, did you hear me?"

I nod but continue standing there.

"Remove your clothes, NOW!" He gnarls through gritted teeth.

I stand trembling, tears pooling in my eyes.

"Are you deliberately disobeying me? That results in punishment, Katherine. I want to redden your ass, but for pleasure; not punishment. Believe me when I say there's a difference."

"I can't," I confess, as tears stream down my cheeks. I drop my eyes to the floor because I can't bear to look him in the eyes. He invades my personal space, lifting my chin.

"Explain to me," he urges, the harshness fading in his voice.

I remember our conversation from Open House, when he wanted my ass bare. I eventually did bare my ass, but most of my body was covered. To say I have body image issues would be an understatement. Taking a deep breath, I try to reason with him. *Who am I kidding? Trying to reason with Isaac Jameson is like trying to reason with a bull in a china shop.*

"I'm plump, fluffy...have rolls...of fat. I've had two kids. I've got stretch marks everywhere; my stomach, my hips, my boobs. I've had C-sections, I have scars. I'm fucking 45 years old," my frustrations reaching their peak.

"Watch your mouth!" Isaac hisses at me. "Are you finished ranting now?"

I remain silent, dropping my eyes back to the floor.

"I take your silence as a yes."

Reaching into the nightstand drawer, he pulls out what looks to be a hunting knife. Fear quickly seizes my heart at the sight of the knife, but dissipates as Isaac repeats his demands.

"Now...undress. Or, I can do it for you," twirling the knife around. "However, I'd rather not ruin your corset because I think you look sexy as hell in it."

I stare at him dumbstruck with my eyes wide and my mouth gaping open.

"NOW!" He roars.

Immediately, I loosen the lacing on the front of the corset. Pulling the elastic sleeves off my shoulders, down my arms; the corset dress puddles on the floor. With Isaac still in possession of my panties from earlier in the night, I stand nervously before him, completely nude.

I will my eyes to meet his, afraid of what I'll see. Expecting to see a repulsiveness lingering there, I'm surprised to see a lustful gleam raking over my body.

Sitting on the bed, he draws me between his legs. He softly caresses from my shoulders down to my breast, heat flaring in its wake. His lips assail my breast, lightly gripping my nipple between his teeth. He continues caressing over my abdomen, tracing every line. I flinch as his hand travels over the plumpness of my belly leading to my sex. He swats my ass hard, leaving a stinging reminder of his hand.

"I know you are submissive Katherine. Your responses to my demands tonight have confirmed my thoughts. I believe you know this, too. Do you want to learn more about your submissiveness?"

Still mesmerized by his touch, I nod in agreement.

"Speak your answer, Katherine? We haven't learned

each other's body language and I don't want any misunderstandings between us."

"Yes, Sir. I do want to learn more, but I'm scared, too," I sigh.

"We all fear what we don't understand. I will teach you about this lifestyle and push your limits. I promise I'll never give you more than you can handle. Your only pain will be pleasure," he assures me. "You will always have your safeword - RED, to stop any scene. Yellow to slow it down. We will take it slow. Are you ready to explore your submissive desires, Katherine?"

What the hell am I doing? I think I've lost my mind. It's a mid-life crisis...that's what it is. He doesn't seem put off by my body, though. Maybe he has bad eyesight. But he could feel the ridges of my stretch marks and scars. There has to be some reason he seems attracted to me.

I'm already going to hell in gasoline soaked panties, so why not...

"Yes, Sir. I'm ready."

"Lay down on your back," he commands and I make my

way onto the bed.

I don't mind lying on my back, as the excess of my body submerges within itself. Though my ample breasts part and gravity pulls them outward.

Isaac parts my legs and kneels between them, stroking his finger over the scar above my mound. Unconsciously, I flinch again and with firm purpose, he smacks the outer part of my thigh.

"Rule number one, don't speak negatively about any part of this body. Right now, it's my body and I don't take kindly to people disrespecting what's mine. You will not hide your body from me.

Rule two, in the club you refer to me as Master; in the bedroom Master or Sir.

Rule three...during your training, you are MINE. You scene with no one without my permission...no one, including other club Masters. You are exclusive to me, as I will be to you. No one touches your body without my permission. You respect me, you respect yourself, at all times. You fuck no one but me. EXCLUSIVE! This encompasses every aspect of your life; whether in the club or not.

Are we clear?" He demands.

"Yes, Sir."

"Good...get on your hands and knees," he smirks with a devilish grin.

Immediately, I'm on my hands and knees. Wasting no time, strands of leather land on my ass. I don't know when or from where he retrieved his leather instrument, but he quickly sets a rhythm lighting fire with every strike on my backside. I begin to pant, as tears well in my eyes. The leather is replaced by his hands rubbing my ass cheeks; warm sensations spreading to my throbbing sex.

Reaching around with his left hand, he kneads my left breast, stroking until his thumb and forefinger clamp on my nipple; pulling and rolling it, sending shockwaves to my clit. His other hand leaves my ass, trailing his fingers through my slick sex, zeroing in on my clit.

"Don't come until I say so, baby," he purrs in my ear.

I groan my displeasure as I writhe under the onslaught of sensation. Pinching and pulling my nipple; his thumb circling and teasing my clit.

"Please...I need to come."

He answers me with a smack to my ass, which only

douses the flame with gasoline.

"Don't beg Katherine. I'll prolong your release," he laughs sadistically.

With relief, he releases my nipple. My reprieve is short lived, as he flips me to my back, pulling my ass to the edge of the bed and buries his tongue in my pussy. He's lapping and nibbling on the lips of my pussy. I'm squirming all over, as I take another swat to my thigh.

"Stay still!" He growls into my mound. "Or the cuffs go on." He releases the pressure on my clit from his thumb, but devours it with his mouth. Sucking it completely inside, then holding the engorged nub between his teeth.

"You taste so fucking good," he hums into my sex.

My heart is pounding in my chest and the room is a bit hazy. My body is consumed by the sensations Isaac is thrusting upon me. I wrench my fingers in his hair, hanging on for dear life. I've never experienced anything like this and the feelings are a bit frightening, but I'd rather die than have him stop.

I hear a rustling sound of sorts. The sensations have come to a halt. I desperately try to focus on my surroundings. My sight zeroes in on Isaac stroking his cock.

"Please, Sir...please. I'm begging," I pant breathlessly.

His smoldering eyes searing me.

"Begging again, little wench?"

"I-I'm sorry...Sir," I breathe. "But...Please, please...."

"Please what, baby?" Staring at me with hooded eyes.

"Fuck me, Sir. Please...it's been so long."

With both hands under my ass, he lifts and drags my ass off the bed impaling me with his thick cock with one hard thrust.

"OH MY GOD!" I scream.

"No, baby. It's not God...It's your Master," he sneers with a chuckle.

Isaac launches a furious pounding to my sex. *I think I'm fucking dreaming. Who gets fucked like this?*

"Don't you come 'til I say so," he teases.

I'm fighting so hard to hang on. Isaac's slowing pace draws me back to reality. I was on the brink, but the slower pace allows me to gain some control back. Isaac gently pushes my bent knees back, as he withdraws most of his cock from my pussy. Missing the fullness, I try to thrust my hips to draw him back in, to no avail.

Slowly thrusting the thick head of his cock just inside my sex, an exhilarating new sensation emerges and pressure builds.

"Oh shit...," I gasp.

"Watch your mouth!"

"Sir, oh my god...what are you doing? Oh my god, oh my...GOD!!!" I scream, shivers pulsating through my body. A chuckle, his only response.

Isaac continues boring into that one spot, that one tantalizing spot.

OH FUCK!!!

My body begins a rolling tremble... "Oh GOD, Oh GOD...Sir. What's happening?"

The pressure is building so rapidly... "IT FEELS SO FUCKING GOOD!!!" I roar.

"Let it go, baby girl...Let it go."

On his order...an eruption shatters my body and a flood escapes me.

I'm drenched. *That can't be from my orgasm.*

Isaac instantly begins pulverizing my pussy, once again. A sloshing sound fills the room. I'm instantly soaring again...the feeling is unimaginable.

A mist hitting my face anchors me back down to Earth. Isaac continues his assault on my sex. The sloshing becomes more prominent, as the mist covers my face and chest. *I'm being sprayed with my own juices.*

Another orgasm overtakes my body as Sir, *my Sir,* roars his own release.

Isaac draws me to his chest and I collapse in his arms. Abruptly, reality dawns in my head that it's very late and I need to go home.

"You're staying here tonight." Isaac murmurs in my ear. "I'm responsible for you now and you are not driving home this late." *I'm beginning to think he CAN read my mind.*

I'm too exhausted to argue and soften into the form of his body. I feel transformed, like a new person in the same body. To the outside world, subjugation mars this relationship; but in reality Isaac has tapped desires that stem from my very core. I've freely given him my submission, conforming to his demands, yet I've never felt more free and more at peace.

His spicy musk scent laced with sex, invades my senses; his hulking arms hold me in a vice, nuzzled into my neck. A girl could get used to this...real quick.

"Can I ask you a question without you thinking I'm stupid?" I whisper into the night.

"I'll never think you're stupid and don't think it about yourself. Need I remind you that your brain is part of this body that belongs to me?" He grouses.

I'm really gonna have to watch my mouth, or my ass will pay the price.

"So your question is...?"

"Um, I've had orgasms before, but I've never experienced ANYTHING like tonight. I soaked a huge spot on your bed. What was that and how did you do it?" I ask in amazement.

"Hmmm...not sure if I want to reveal my secrets," he teases.

"Well, you are supposed to be teaching me?" I tease back, half expecting a swat to my ass.

"Since you put it like that... I'll share. I was thrusting in on your G-spot which caused you to squirt," He replies amusingly.

"Squirt???" I ask bewildered.

"Squirting is what female ejaculation is called, different than a vaginal or clitoral orgasm. Few women experience it, only because they don't allow their body to relax enough. When most women get the urge, they think they have to urinate. So they don't allow themselves to let go, so they don't experience it. Think of it as a higher level of orgasm. It was a first for me, too," He explains as he nips my neck.

"Squirting, huh? Who knew?"

****

Isaac

I never realized how much I would love waking up and burying myself balls deep, in a warm, wet pussy. Never experienced it with my ex-wife, she was such a bitch in the morning and I've never spent the night with subs. *So why the fuck are you doing it now?*

Katherine didn't resist at all, just submitted to me even

before she was fully aware of what I was doing; a natural sub.

She felt so good; stroking her pussy soft and slow, then her clenching my cock with her release. I love feeling her soft body next to mine. I could get lost in her. I could get used to waking up like this.

What am I doing??? Fuck...

Chapter 13

Thank heavens this day is almost over. Skipping lunch makes for a very long day, but I need to get out of here early to open Nexus for Isaac. I can't believe I've been there four weeks already. I really can't believe my ass has survived four weeks of training with Isaac. It's finally sinking in that he says what he means and means what he says. Cursing and sarcasm are my most recurring offenses. I guess the old saying 'you can't teach an old dog new tricks' is probably true.

Four weeks of submissive training...four weeks of riding an emotional roller coaster. I've always had wicked desires of being bound; at the mercy of a lover with a healthy dose of possessiveness and submitting to his every need. I thought of them as fantasies. But the last four weeks have taught me that I have a deep seeded desire to please. Peace and serenity fill my heart with my submission. It is the core of my being. Isaac has taught me that submission doesn't mean weakness; it actually is a sign of great strength and courage. Trusting one so completely, that you relinquish control of your heart, mind, body, and soul to them; knowing they will cherish you and your gift.

I've known my pain threshold is high, but the immense pleasure that encompasses me through the pain is unimaginable. Many times, elevating me to a state of euphoria.

At times, Isaac is very professional and distant; showing little emotion. Business like...sans the fuck-tacular sex. Then at other times, he removes his Kevlar exterior and I feel as though our souls kiss. My mind suffers from whiplash...*so does my heart.*

NO, dumbass, no heart shit...this is strictly training, strictly business. He made it very clear...with his words. And I know I'm going to get hurt when this little business partnership is over.

"So I hear I'll be joining you on the trip to Chicago next week," Rick boasts as he sits on my desk, drawing me from my thoughts. I shoot an evil glare at him in response and he immediately stands. "So...you, me, a hotel, overnight," he suggests in the most vile manner possible. *That's all I need...his sleazy ass on an overnight business trip. Jeezus...can this day get any worse.*

"Business, Rick...business," I reply stoically. I'll definitely make sure Jean books our rooms on separate floors.

Separate hotels would be better...but that's not likely.

I quickly gather my things, dismissing Rick completely. The cleaning crew will be waiting on me at Nexus, if I don't get a move on. Of all days for Isaac to be out of town and Patrick to be on duty. I guess it was bound to happen that both of them would be away from the club at the same time, sooner or later.

Thankfully, I arrive before the cleaning crew, as they pull up just as I get inside. Since Isaac is not here, I'll be sticking close to the office and lobby tonight. Along with his list of 'do's and don'ts', he's given me permission to dress in my regular work clothes tonight; no corsets. *Thank goodness!*

By the time I get everything prepped and ready to open, the cleaning crew has left and staff is arriving. I've never been in the club without Isaac being here. It'll certainly be different without him. He's only been gone a couple of days, but I miss him. *No, no, no...you don't miss him.* However, he does make great use of video chat.

It's usually the same members on Thursday nights, so we should be fine. Thankfully Derek will be here to help out, since Patrick is away, too. Tiny will work security at the door, Gina at the sign in counter and Zeke will be bartending.

I decide to try and get a little ahead with the paperwork tonight since I'll be out of town a couple days next week, plus I won't be scening with Isaac tonight so I should have some extra time. Though most of our scenes occur in his bedroom, not the club. I get to work reconciling the bank statement. The loud ding from my phone alerts of incoming video chat.

"Hello, Sir. How was your day?"

"Better now, that I see my Peaches. Are you in the office?"

"Yes, Sir."

"Close the door and lock it. Then come back and have a seat in the chair."

I do as he instructed.

"Door's locked."

"Good. Now, open the stand on the back of your phone and sit your phone on the desk."

I adjust the phone so that we can see each other.

"Okay...I see you, can you see me okay?"

"Perfect! Now open the top side drawer. I left you something."

I open the drawer and there's a long, black rectangular box with my name on it. I quickly open it to find a new toy and a packet of lubricant. My sex instantly begins to throb.

"It's a dual vibrator for your clit and G-spot. Are you wearing a skirt like I asked?"

"Yes." I reply with my breath catching in my throat.

"Now, take off your panties and insert your new toy. I want to watch you come, Peaches," his husky moan causing my body to tremble.

I quickly apply lubricant to both phalluses, inserting the larger one just inside my sex, while resting the shorter one up against my clit. The hum immediately causes the pressure to build in my pussy. I check to make sure he can see as he hasn't spoken in the past couple of minutes. I'm startled to see his hand gripping this thick cock, stroking it slowly.

I adjust the intensity and rhythm of my new toy and a moan escapes my lips. My eyes close as I roll my head back on the chair. My hips automatically began grinding the vibrating toy. My orgasm is building rapidly.

"Oh, Sir...it feels so good. I want you, Sir. God...how I want you," I cry out.

"That's my girl. You're free to come anytime, Peaches."

At his encouragement, I apply more pressure on my clit. My orgasm explodes through my body as I try to swallow my screams of release.

"FUUUCK!" Roars from my phone and I witness Isaac's release by his own hand.

I'm a little shocked at my arousal of seeing that, just shortly after my own shattering release.

I grab some tissues to clean myself as Isaac is doing the same, taking a couple moments to regain my composure.

"Thank you, Sir. For my gift and my orgasm," I giggle.

"It was very much my pleasure, Peaches. I only wish I was there to continue."

"Oh, by the way, I have to go to Chicago next week for business. I'll be gone overnight Tuesday, fly back Wednesday afternoon," I announce.

Silence briefly fills the air, as Isaac appears to be pondering a thought.

"Hmmm...I may have to come back here next Wednesday. If I do, I'll change it to Tuesday, so we're out of town at the same time. Otherwise, we won't see each other most of the week. We're just finding our rhythm with your training. I don't want to disrupt it if we don't have to," he explains.

I can't believe he would change his schedule for me. It makes my heart smile.

"Are you traveling alone to Chicago?" He inquires.

"Unfortunately, not," I grumble.

"Why is it unfortunate?"

"The salesman for the account is going, too. I'm not very fond of him. That's all."

"Him???" He repeats and I see his jaw clench.

"Yes, Sir... Rick Foster. He can be a jerk, at times," I explain, trying to ease the tension I see in his face, but with nothing really nice to say about Rick, I think I'm making it worse.

"I asked Jean to book us on separate floors."

Damn...that made his jaw clench tighter. *Shit!*

"He bothers you so much, you want rooms on separate floors?" His questions nearing interrogation level.

“It’s fine, really. He’s just obnoxious.” *I need to shut up!*

“We’ll discuss it more when I get home. I should be in tomorrow afternoon and we can discuss it over dinner,” he directs.

“Sounds good. I look forward to seeing you,” I smile, trying to lighten his sudden dark mood. *Damn, that sounded a little desperate...*

“Same here, Peaches. Call me when you get home tonight, so I know you made it home safe.”

“Sure thing, Sir.”

I set to task organizing the files to correspond with the changes I’ve made to the accounting system. Hopefully, it will make it easier on the next person, to keep everything current. My heart clinches at that thought. *The next person. His next sub. Get a grip, Kathy, you’re not staying here forever. He WILL get another sub, several more...I’m sure.*

Mumbled voices outside the office door draw my attention away from my irrational thoughts. The office door suddenly swings open.

“Hey baby, I’m ba-......who the hell are you and where’s my master?” Demanded the model thin blonde, standing in the doorway.

When I stood, I could see Gina standing behind the woman, who was clearly looking for Isaac. The woman was a tad shorter than me. A body that looks like she hasn't eaten an ounce of sugar in her life and an unnatural rack that causes her body to struggle to stay balanced.

"May I help you?" I offer with a smile. Trying to keep my emotions in check.

"Who are you?" The woman demands again.

"I'm Kathy. Can I help you?"

"Where's Isaac...my master?" She snaps.

"Isaac is not here. Is there something I can help you with?" I reply, straining to keep my cool.

"Unless you have a fat cock, I don't think YOU can help me," She snobs with her hands on her thin hips, jutting out her inflated breasts.

"Why are you in his office? At his desk?" Her shrilling voice piercing my ears.

"Kathy, I tried to explain to *Vickie* that Master Isaac wasn't here, but she barged past me anyway," Gina interrupts, shooting daggers with her eyes in the woman's back.

The woman I now know is Vickie, Isaac's former sub. *Fucking great...this is fucking great. Obviously, the day can get worse.*

"I can take a message and leave it for Isaac, if you like, but he won't be in tonight."

The woman, *Vickie,* laughs out loud and rolls her eyes.

"A message...seriously??? Just give me his number, I'll call him myself," she says in a bitchy tone.

"That's personal information that I'm not at liberty to divulge." *That and it would be a cold day in hell before I would anyway.*

"Just give me the god damn number, so I can leave," she shrieks.

A small chuckle escapes my lips as my heart begins to pound. *I'm 'bout to lose my shit!!! Keep it together, Kathy. This is a place of business, a job you need this summer, until Ben returns from France. Steeling my nerves...*

"Vickie, is it? Let me be clear. I can leave a message for Mr. Jameson, if you like. Otherwise, we are done here and you can see yourself out." My words coated thick with ice.

"You can't kick me out. This is Isaac's office!"

"Well, you see...that's where you're wrong. This is my office, too. Isaac and I share it. So yeah...I CAN kick you out and I'm doing just that," I sneer with clenched fists.

"I'll talk with my master about this!"

Master...master... If she says "her master" one more time, I'm gonna knock her the fuck out.

"You do that...," I threaten.

Fury's strumming through my veins. I take some deep breaths to calm my nerves. That condescending, presumptuous bitch. Barging in here like she belongs. *Hell...what do I know? Maybe she does. I don't know their arrangement. How they ended things? If they ended things, for good. Stop it, right now. He is exclusive to me, at least during my training. She didn't know how to reach him, wanted me to give her his number. So she couldn't have had any recent contact with him. But...why is she back? What does she want?* Doubt creeping in as it always does.

I wrap things up in the office, ready to call it a night. I console Gina, as she's wracked with shame, that she let Vickie get past her tonight. It was apparent Vickie was on a mission and no one was going to stand in her way.

Barely in the house, I strip out of my bra and heels. Dying for a hot shower, I decide to wait to call Isaac once I get out.

T-shirt on and wine in hand, I grab my phone to call Isaac, when his thunderous ringtone startles me.

"Hey, Si.."

"WHERE THE FUCK HAVE YOU BEEN?" Isaac roars, interrupting my greeting.

"At the club. Why? What's wrong?"

"Why haven't you called?" Anger lacing his words.

"I just picked up the phone to call, Sir," I tried to coax him with his title.

"I expected a call over 30 minutes ago. I've been calling you and you didn't answer. I've been worried sick. I called Derek and he said y'all left almost an hour ago," he continues to rant.

"I'm sorry, Sir. I was so eager to get comfortable and get a hot shower, I decided to call you afterwards," I plea my case.

"I told you to call me when you got home, so I knew you were safe. You purposely disobeyed me, Katherine."

Katherine...I don't like when he calls me Katherine. I love for him to call me "Peaches"... Not Katherine! He's definitely pissed.

"I'm so sorry. It will never happen again, Sir."

"Damn right, it won't," he growls with a threatening tone.

I'm sure my ass will pay for this little slip up.

After an extended moment of silence, our conversation continues.

"How was it tonight?" He asks in a much calmer voice.

"Everything went well, I think. I organized the files and reconciled your bank statement. Trying to get ahead, so I don't fall behind next week when I'm out of town."

"Ah...yes. Chicago. We'll discuss your trip when I get home tomorrow, to plan our week."

"That sounds great," I reply excitedly.

"Oh, by the way...someone came by Nexus to see you tonight." *I really had almost forgot, after his tirade about me not calling.*

"A woman named...*Vickie*."

****

Isaac

What is that conniving bitch up to? I told her to stay away from Nexus, stay away from me. Katherine admitted she asked Vickie to leave, but didn't elaborate. Best not to push the issue over the phone, I'd rather talk about what happened, face to face. But I wonder how bad it got.

Katherine seemed pretty calm when she told me the bitch came by, but knowing what an instigator Vickie is, I can only imagine it got ugly. Especially, if it pushed Peaches to kick her out.

I don't want Vickie and her drama infiltrating the club again. I was so blind to her malicious antics before, because I kept her at arm's length, not letting her get close. But because of that tactic, I failed to see the shit storm she was causing right under my nose. It almost cost me some good friends and the club. A mistake I won't let happen again.

Exactly why you need to keep your head straight with Katherine, dumbass.

Chapter 14

This morning is dragging by. Usually Fridays fly, but not today. I'm anxious to meet Deb for lunch to talk over this *Vickie* bullshit. I tend to go with my gut feeling about situations like this, *and my gut says that bitch is trouble,* but it's always nice to bounce my thoughts off Deb. I'm curious as to what her reaction will be.

I'm also a little antsy about dinner with Isaac tonight. We're supposed to discuss my trip to Chicago. I sensed some apprehension from him when I told him about it and he mentioned it again last night that we would "talk" about it when he gets back in town. And by no means am I foolish enough to believe that he accepted my nonchalant reaction to the *Vickie* situation. He questions my feelings about *EVERYTHING,* but he didn't grill me about *why* I kicked her out. *Didn't seem surprised I did it, either, come to think about it.* Maybe he was just consumed with his own anger, 'cause there was lots of growling and cursing going on.

A little before noon, I grab my purse and head toward

the elevator. On the ride down, I overhear two ladies from the sales department talking about what a sleaze Rick is and one spoke about how he had grabbed her ass in the break room. I take a deep breath and exhale to help rid the dread filling my gut. I see the crap that goes on here, I can only imagine how bold he'll be out of town. *Shit...*

I make my way to Delancey's. Thankfully Deb has secured us a booth cause this place is packed.

"Hey chicka," I call out as I slide in the seat. I love our lunch get togethers. We talk a lot, but our *real* talks; the life changing, decision making talks always seem to happen over lunch. Deb's suspicions of her cheating husband, her decision to leave her husband. Trying to rationalize the volatile fights with my ex, and like her, my decision that enough was enough and my ex had to go... all over lunch.

"Hey, girlie. How's your day going?" She replies sipping her tea. "When will Isaac be back?"

"This evening, sometime. We're supposed to have dinner."

"Dinner, huh? So, how did it go at the club last night without him there? Bet it was strange."

"Funny you ask. He had a visitor stop by to see him last

night."

"Really... Who???" She asks with a raised brow.

"His former sub," I simper.

"What?!?!" Deb wails back. "What did she want?"

"Isaac."

"Why? Did she say why?" Deb implores with increasing insistence.

"She kept referring to him as "her master"? I wanted to bust her right in the mouth."

"Like in the present tense. Like he was her master, now!" Deb's voice began to elevate.

"Shhh, keep it down." I glare at her. Deb can get quite animated when she gets emotional.

"Yes...she was talking in the present tense. She also pushed my buttons, to the point I kicked her out...tactfully. She's a bitch and I'd had enough of her mouth. If she hadn't left, I'm not sure I would've stayed in control."

"Did you tell Isaac?"

"Yes. He was quite upset. I didn't go into details on the

phone, but that's one of the things I'm sure we'll discuss tonight, along with my trip to Chicago."

"So what do you think she wants?"

"I don't know. My mind was all over the place last night. My gut tells me she's trouble and my gut never lies."

"What's up with your trip to Chicago?"

"I'm not sure, to tell the truth. Isaac seemed to get uptight when I told him about the trip. He mentioned again on the phone last night that we would discuss my trip when he got home. Guess I'll find out tonight."

The afternoon is dragging by much like the morning did. I bury myself in prepping for the Chicago presentation.

"Hey, what do you say we grab a drink after work to discuss our trip?" Rick's voice startles me. *At least he didn't sit on my desk.*

"Sorry...I have plans. Besides, there's nothing for us to discuss, nothing the team hasn't already talked about repeatedly." I'm direct, but with a cordial tone.

Rick moves behind my chair and leans down to my ear.

"I wasn't talking about the presentation, babe. I want to discuss our after-hour plans," the words sliming from his lips.

A chill slides down my back, but fury fortifies my spine. Without thinking, I shove my chair back, almost a direct hit into him. I catapult out of my chair, coming within an inch of his ruddy face, pointing my finger in his chest.

"First of all, I'm not your *BABE!!!* Secondly, there will be no *after-hour* plans." I scathe. *I am shaking with fury, remembering the conversation I overheard in the elevator. I need to calm down before I'm the one written up.* I take a deep breath to calm my nerves.

"Now, stop with this mess. Seriously Rick... just stop. You have a wife and family. You should have more respect for them," I chastise.

A chirp from my phone draws my attention momentarily away from Rick and thankfully, he trudges off. I grab my phone and see it's a text from Isaac.

Isaac: How's your day going?

Me: Good...how bout yours?

Certainly not getting into the confrontation with Rick through text. Texting's great for quick messages and such, but more often than not, people are misunderstood. You can't see their face or hear their tone so you're not sure of their mood or intent.

Isaac: Better as the day goes on. Closer to sinking balls deep into your wet pussy.

My clit begins to throb just at his typed words. I'm so pathetic...

Me: Ummm... YES...please!

Isaac: Plan to get dressed for the club at my place.

Me: Yes, Sir!

Isaac: I should be home by 6pm. Can you be there then?

Me: I should...if traffic cooperates. I need to run home after work, grab my things, and I'll be on my way.

Isaac: Be safe.

Me: Will do. You, too.

That little text exchange went a long way in dissipating my anger with Rick. Isaac has a way of calming me, which is kind of an oxymoron, considering how uptight he can get about some things. *My sassy mouth, for example.*

Wrapping up the day, I stroll to the elevator to make my exodus along with the rest. The hair on the back of my neck suddenly stands on end. My peripheral vision snags a glimpse of Rick standing just to my left shoulder. *Shit…I don't want to ride the elevator down with him. At least I won't be alone with him. That would be awkward after our little tiff this afternoon.*

Thankfully, the elevator is full and we're on opposite sides. The elevator door opens on the lobby floor and I immediately step out. Rick steps off and brushes my shoulder with his arm draped over a woman's shoulder. As he's sauntering away he turns back toward me.

"Have fun with your plans," he smirks with a sardonic laugh.

What the hell is wrong with him? I shake my head in disbelief, ready to end this day.

****

Driving down the canopied driveway of Nexus in daylight, always takes my breath away. It's like being transported to another place in time; to an antebellum, Gone with the Wind era. It's so beautiful...

I pull around to the unmarked drive to the left and park in Isaac's residence driveway. My heart is thrumming in my chest. I hate admitting it, but I missed him. I know realistically this is going nowhere. It's an arrangement, a learning experience, but I'm growing attached to Isaac in spite of myself. I know in the end, my heart will break.

I softly knock on his door, staring aimlessly at the beautiful surroundings. The door opens and instantly my mouth is besieged by Isaac's. Grasping a handful of my hair, pulling me across the threshold, his tongue willfully invades my lips and plunders my mouth until every crevice has been seared by his touch. My body immediately surrenders to him.

Ripping his mouth from mine, he slams the door and pierces me with a feral glare.

"Strip...," he commands.

I falter for a moment, under his hypnotic stare. I know he said something, but for the life of me I can't recall quick enough.

"Now!" He growls, causing me to jump clear out of my skin.

I drop my overnight bag and immediately unfasten my skirt, shimmying it down my legs. I begin unbuttoning my blouse, my eyes never leaving his. I believe I see a slight tremor below his skin. Closing the distance between us in one lunge, buttons ping across the floor as his patience snaps and he rips my blouse open. Just as swift, his hand frees my left breast from its harness of black lace. He palms my breast as he devours my mouth once again. He grazes his way along my jaw, nibbling a trail to the soft, fleshy area on my neck. I'm squirming under the sensation.

"Be still!" Isaac growls into my neck as he bites the sensitive area between my neck and shoulder, pulsating to my sex, all the while pulling and elongating my hardened nub.

I'm fighting to stay in control, as Isaac makes his way to my left breast, lavishing the beaded area with wicked flicks of his tongue before gripping the beaded crux between his teeth. Delicious pulsating sensations rivet straight to my clit. His tongue softens and soothes the ravaged area before pulling away.

"On your knees...I want to feel your succulent lips at the base of my cock, Peaches."

I immediately drop to my knees, unfastening his jeans, freeing his magnificent cock. I graze my fingers over his shorn sac, cupping them as I inhale the blend of spice and musk enticing my pilgrimage up his delectable shaft. A dewy drop of his essence awaits me at my summit. I swirl my tongue around, prolonging my reward.

"Damn girl…you're killing me." Isaac groans fisting my hair.

It's a heady feeling knowing I'm bringing him to the brink of losing control. A faint smile emerges on my lips. The tip of my tongue breaches his slit as I partake in my reward glistening on the thick head of his cock. I coat the head before trailing my tongue down the thick veins along the side of his shaft, around the base and up again. I feel his tremor as I lick around the smooth head, sucking it into my mouth. I hear Isaac inhale a rugged breath through clenched teeth. In one quick stroke I take him to the back of my throat, repeating it over and over. Licking, sucking, worshipping his delicious shaft. I'm so aroused sucking his cock, my clit is throbbing. I'm on the verge of coming. I slightly shift and my folds graze my engorged clit, sending me over the edge, moaning over his cock as my wetness seeps from my folds.

"FUCK!!!" Isaac growls fisting both hands in my hair, as he begins impaling the back of my throat with every thrust. As debase as the act must appear, it is erotically thrilling to me.

Complete surrender.

Isaac slows his thrusts as I feel him swell thicker in my mouth. My signal he's on the verge of release. After a few more hard thrusts, he erupts.

"Take it all, baby. Take all of me...FUUUCK!!!"

His warm, salty essence pulses down my throat. I quickly swallow, so not to gag. *Something I've learned during my training with Isaac. I had some embarrassing moments in the beginning; choking, gagging, spewing. Not much practice with the ex. But Isaac has been quite patient.*

Lifting me to my feet, Isaac gathers me in his arms, nuzzling his face in my neck. With a handful of my hair, he tugs my face to his gaze.

"Thank you, Peaches." He says kissing my forehead, then kissing my mouth, biting my lower lip.

Unable to avert my gaze from his, I need to tell him of my little indiscretion. *Or I couldn't. I could clean up and he'd be none the wiser. Or he could run his fingers between my sex now and he'd definitely know.*

"Sir, I-I...I'm sorry. I broke a rule," I stammer.

"What rule did you break?" He asks with a raised brow.

"I, um... I had an orgasm without your permission, Sir."

"And when did this indiscretion occur?" He asks with a slight smile.

"Ummm...just a bit ago. While I was sucking your cock, Sir," I whisper.

A roaring laugh rips from his throat. I stand here assessing his outburst. *I'm not sure if he's laughing because he's gonna whip my ass, he thinks I'm pathetic, or what?*

"I just couldn't stop myself. I get so aroused sometimes, that I just climax," I try explaining.

"I appreciate your honesty, baby. I lost control myself, tonight, so we'll call it even. I just had to get my hands on you. I'll replace your shirt. I'm sure I ruined it."

"Yes, Sir...I think you did," I laugh.

Chapter 15

While I showered, Isaac finished preparing dinner; caramelized salmon, grilled California blend, and a crisp salad. I've never had salmon, but I try making a believable attempt to eat it. I won't be rude and not eat, but much to my surprise the salmon is delicious.

Wearing a robe that was hanging on the back of the bathroom door, I'm surrounded by Isaac's spicy scent. Although the belt is snuggly tied, the top repeatedly falls open exposing most of my breasts. A smirk sits on Isaac's lips. I'm not sure if he's enjoying the view or my struggle keeping the robe closed.

"So talk to me about your upcoming trip," Isaac inquires.

I've thought about this impending conversation all day. Unsure of what he would ask, I ran different scenarios through my mind, but never quite coming up with a response to any of them. However, I do know Isaac picked up on my anxiety when I first told him about the trip.

"Not much to say...it's just a sales presentation to a new client." I reply in between bites, not making eye contact.

"I see..."

I feel his glare on my face as I pick at my food, not wanting to meet his eyes. Moments later, I literally feel a cooling sensation across my cheeks and I know he has looked away, though not speaking a word. His silence is calling to my soul, urging it to bare its secret concerns. God, I think I'd rather him yell.

"Well...," I begin. "Like I told you the other day, Rick is a little obnoxious, a lot obnoxious. He's quite perfidious. He's a married man, yet he has trouble keeping his hands to himself."

I see Isaac's jaw twitching. *You just had to spill your guts...* I sneak a peek at his eyes and my tummy flips. His eyes are dark and sinister. *Why am I telling him this? He wasn't saying a word...just sitting quietly. I should've left well enough alone.*

"He's just a flirt. I've set him straight and clearly established my boundaries," I blurt out breaking the silence and infuriating Isaac even more, though he still hasn't uttered a word. I should be basking in his silence, but it just compels me to reveal more.

"Has he ever put his hands on you?" He asks with a glacial tone.

Oh shit...think Katherine, think. Carefully gather your words...I'm not going to lie, but I don't want Isaac to explode and he looks like that could be possible. Rick's grabbed my ass once, but after threatening him, he's never touched me again. It's his creepy comments that make my skin crawl.

"Your silence is speaking very loud, Peaches." His words thawed...a little.

"Yes...once" I whisper, my heart pounding. "And I threatened to break his wrist if it happened again."

A howl of laughter broke from his chest, calming my nerves and easing the tension in the room.

"That's my girl....," he beams.

"So, has he treated you negatively since?" He continues.

"Yes and no." My remark causing his eyebrow to raise in question.

"I mean...no, he hasn't touched me again. And no, he

hasn't spoken negative words to me. But sometimes his words make me feel uncomfortable. He uses monikers with women, myself included, which should be reserved for his wife. I've told him as much, too. He's grossly flirtatious with most women. His behavior is sickening as it is, but knowing he's married with children...it makes it worse. I think the only reason no one has reported him to human resources is out of empathy for his wife and kids; afraid he'll lose his job," I ramble on as the flood gate is wide open.

"So my apprehension about the trip is that I don't like his personality. I don't like being around the obnoxiousness. That's all," I conclude.

"My only contact with him on the trip should remain in the meeting only. No socializing afterward," I reassure him.

"Good. Keep it that way," He demands.

Clearing the table, I decide to turn the interrogation on him.

"Who is Vickie?" I state. I tried to be casual but it came out quite blunt. Not sure how this is gonna go, I don't push the conversation, allowing Isaac to guide it...for now. He remains quiet, though his brows are furrowed and his jaw clenched. I carry my dishes to the sink and begin rinsing them to fill the lull in conversation.

"She was my sub. I released her over a year ago," he offers with a pained look on his face.

I'm not sure how to read that look. I've never seen it before. His expression is wrought with sorrow and anger. Maybe he misses her…angry that she left. But he said *he* released her. Throwing caution to the wind and possibly my ass too, I continue with my inquisition.

"May I ask why?"

"Inquisitive, are we?" He smirks.

"Curious, I guess."

"You know what curiosity did to the cat, don't you?" Pinning me with a steely glare.

"Killed it. But I don't think you'll kill me."

"No Peaches, I won't kill you. Blister your ass? Now, that's possible."

A shiver runs down my spine, as dampness emerges between my thighs.

"She referred to you as her Master," I murmur.

"I am NOT her master," he growls.

Shaking his head, he pauses and takes a deep breath, exhaling in a puff.

"She became, probably always was...conniving, manipulative, and deceitful. I misjudged her submission. I was not a good master to her. A true master would have been more aware of her behaviors and corrected them or released her sooner. I was not invested in the relationship, therefore I missed signs that were glaring in front of my face."

His damning admission leaves me weak in the knees. Words have left me and I stand here, stunned.

"It's the reason I don't have a permanent sub now. You must be invested in any relationship for it to work, but it's the basis of a D/s relationship," he confesses.

My heart seizes at his declaration. *Will he ever have another permanent sub?* I'm dying to ask him, but I don't know if I can handle his answer.

A slap to my ass draws my attention back to the here and now.

"Go get dressed, Peaches. It's about time to head down to the club."

****

Walking downstairs, I keep pulling down on the black Lycra skirt I'm wearing. I should've tried it on. It looked long enough when I held it up against me. Obviously I didn't account for the skirt having to stretch over my fat ass and hips, that shortened it a couple of inches. Now I think the flab on my inner thighs is showing below the skirt. My corset is preventing me from getting a good look to see for sure. Every time I bend over to see, the skirt comes up obscenely more.

My pulling and tugging has caught Isaac's attention, as he smacks my hand away from my skirt. At the bottom of the stairs, he thrusts me against the door that leads into Nexus. Gripping my chin with his left hand, my body immediately tenses. His right hand easily maneuvers my skirt up, rolling it to my waist. His free hand begins groping the cheeks of my ass, the calloused feeling sparking electricity to my clit.

"What's the problem, Peaches?" He breathes onto my lips.

"Just trying to pull my skirt down, Sir. It's shorter than I thought."

"The skirt is perfect and you look fucking amazing in it. I love how it allows me easy access to feel this luscious ass that belongs to me. No fighting with keeping it out of my way. It stays exactly where I want it to, giving me ample access to this pussy. This pussy that is MINE!" He groans, as he dips between my folds, sinking one, then two fingers deep in my sex.

He hungrily takes my mouth while he slowly strokes in and out of my sex. I relax into him, my body submitting completely.

Withdrawing his fingers, he tears his mouth from mine. Bringing his glistening fingers to his mouth, licking them clean.

"I needed a little taste to tie me over until I devour your pussy later," he whispers with a wicked grin.

"Now, enough with the skirt," he smacks my ass before rolling the skirt back in place.

We make our way into Nexus. I head to the office to get started on the books, while Isaac checks on the activities in the club.

****

Isaac

"What'll you have, Ike?" Zeke asks as I lean on the bar.

"Just a water, man...no, make it a beer."

"The usual?" Zeke calls back over his shoulder

"That'll do."

I grab a stool, as I try to sort through the events of the day.

She's lucky she's still wearing a skirt, because I came close to ripping it off her ass. I've warned her about belittling herself and the consequences of doing so. She's smart...I give her that. She didn't say anything negative, but her actions speak louder than her words. I don't know what her problem is anyway. She's fucking gorgeous. Her face is smooth as porcelain, beautiful plump lips that I love to bite, her eyes are grey one minute and green the next. I drown in her eyes when I bury deep in her wet pussy; her eyes are most definitely green when she comes all over me.

Her ass... firm and round. Damn, my cock hardens at the thought. Her tits are perfect. Soft and supple, like the rest of her body. When I hold a woman, I want her to feel like a woman; soft, smooth, curvy. I'm a powerful man who plays rough. I need a woman that can endure the deviant things I want to do to her body. Peaches is perfect for my kinda play.

What's up with the little fucker at her job? I'm not thrilled about Peaches going on this business trip. It's work and I can't stop her, but I don't like it. She seems to have handled this guy's crap, so far, but being 800 miles away with him leaves her vulnerable. She's my sub, in training, but it's still my job to protect her and I can't 800 miles away. If that prick so much as looks at her the wrong way, I rip his fucking head off and spit down his throat.

I still need to find out what the hell Vickie is up to and why the hell she's coming around here. I told her to stay away. Stupid bitch never listened. Now, she's involved Katherine in whatever scheme she's up to, putting me in an awkward situation of having to tell her about the sordid details of releasing Vickie and how I failed at being her master. Truth be told, I probably shouldn't be training Katherine. But training them is not a problem, being a Master to them...well, that's another story.

It's a busy night, so I finish my beer and decide to go check on some scenes.

Chapter 16

Giving my eyes a break from the computer screen, I walk out to the front desk to chat with Gina.

"How's it looking tonight, Gina?"

"Busy, girl...busy. GUESS WHAT?!?!? We have some VIPs in the house tonight," Gina's voice rising to a squeal.

"Really...who?"

"Do you remember Derek telling us about some big time actor that would be in Atlanta filming for a month or so, and wanted to visit Nexus? Well, he's here...tonight. And he's a HOTTIE!"

I didn't think Gina's voice could go any higher, but I think she could shatter glass with it.

"That's exciting! I may have to take a stroll and check out some scenes tonight," I tilt my head with a smirk.

"Oooo...maybe Derek can watch the desk for a bit and I can stroll with you." Gina muses clapping her hands, doing the 'happy dance'.

"Maybe... if you ask nicely," I tease.

"As if there's another way to ask around here." Gina chuckles.

"Gina, is my skirt long enough? Does it cover the flab on my inner thighs? I can't really tell. When I bend over to look, the skirt comes up higher," I ask pulling on my skirt again.

"It looks fine to me. You look beautiful," She offers with a smile.

"Thanks hon, you're sweet to say that. It's just been a little challenging for me to wear club attire. I'm not used to revealing so much of myself. If I had a body like yours, I wouldn't mind flaunting my goodies; but I'm very self-conscious about my flabby body. Nobody wants to see my size 18 body flitting around in a corset with my ass hanging out," I chide.

Gina's smile quickly disappears from her face. Before I can register the reason, a massive hand grips my arm like a vice and my skirt's yanked up to my waist.

"You mean hanging out like this?" Isaac chuckles.

I try spinning around to face him, but I'm in an

awkward position. I grab at my skirt with my free hand, trying to cover my bare ass. Isaac slaps my hand away.

"What are you doing?" I hiss, as my temper flares.

"Any damn thing I want to," he snaps back.

"Put my skirt back down," I demand gritting my teeth, momentarily forgetting where I am and who I'm talking to.

"You need to remember who the fuck you're talking to. Do you need a reminder?" Isaac snarls, gripping my arm tighter; striking my ass hard.

My breath catching in my throat and tears welling in my eyes, as the searing pain spreads. That was not for pleasure. Isaac said I will know the difference when it happens, and he was right.

"I'm sorry Master." I whisper as a pooling tear streaks down my cheek.

"My temper got the better of me. Please forgive me for disrespecting you," I plea.

"I know there's a little hellcat inside you, Peaches. I'm glad I finally got to see it," he chuckles.

"Your sassy mouth is not the problem. You are typically

very respectful. However, you continue to thumb your nose at Rule number one - You are NOT to speak negatively of your body. You are degrading what's MINE and that…is disrespectful. You will be punished."

Punished? Damn, didn't he just blister my ass? Oh, hell.

"Where's Gina?" He asks, slightly irritated.

"She was just here," I offer. *My guess is she made herself scarce when I popped off at Isaac.*

"She's always disappearing. She's supposed to be at the desk," Isaac huffs.

Just then, Gina comes around the corner, explaining to Isaac she went to the ladies' room.

"Stay at the desk, Gina. Katherine will be with me," Isaac orders, grabbing my hand and pulling me along behind him. *So much for checking out the hottie actor scening.*

"Sir, where are we going?" I ask trotting behind him.

Abruptly we stop, Isaac turning toward me glaring.

"Do you need a refresher in all of the rules, Peaches?"

I pause to consider his question. *What did I do? Or*

say…ooops. Master, in the club.

"No, Master Isaac. No refresher is needed."

Isaac continues leading me down the hall toward the theme rooms, apprehension coursing through my veins. I haven't been in any of the theme rooms. Well I have, but not to scene, just walking through them. As a diversion from my uneasiness, I scan the different scenes looking for an unfamiliar face; the hottie actor, but no such luck. We stop at the 'Exam Room' and my heart begins to pound. *No, no, no…not here.* Isaac opens the door and ushers me in, closing the door behind him. *Oh, shit…*

The room is stark white, very cold and sterile; much like that of a real doctor's office. Cabinets, drawers, a sink, and a flexible lamp fill the room. In the center of the room, in all its glory is an exam table; fashioned with stirrups, of course. A seemingly normal exam room in an abnormal location. A closer look at the exam table reveals some alterations. D rings have been bolted along the sides and two leather straps with buckles.

A moist kiss on the back of my neck startles me. Isaac trails kisses intermingled with nibbles across my neck and shoulders, while reaching around unhooking the front of my corset until it drops to the floor. His trail descends down my spine, each bite sending a bolt of electricity straight to my clit. His hands ease the elastic skirt over my hips and down my legs, topping the corset on the floor. Isaac's hands grip each of my hips, drawing his tongue along the crevice of my ass cheeks. My legs are quivering so; I can hardly keep my balance. My sex is drenched, seeping between my folds. My body is trembling with desire, my mind floating away. Sinking his teeth into the flesh of my ass, Isaac draws me back to my senses, as a squeal escapes my lips.

Isaac stands and retrieves something from the counter. I notice several items laid out. Isaac must have pulled them from the drawers while I took in the sights of the room

"Hold out your hands," Isaac requests.

Arms outstretched, Isaac straps leather cuffs on each wrist and bends to strap one on each of my ankles. He guides me over to the exam table, attaching each wrist cuff to a D ring on each side of my head. The table is inclined about forty-five degrees, so I'm in a leaning back position; not lying flat. He takes my feet, placing each one in a stirrup and attaching the ankle cuff to it. He brings a strap over my plump belly immobilizing me completely. A flutter begins at my core, radiating throughout my body. Bound and completely open, I'm at his mercy.

"I have a surprise for you Peaches," he utters across my lips, sending a shiver down my spine.

On a metal tray beside the table, I see several bell shaped devices of varying sizes. They appear to be made of glass. A cylinder shaped tool, similar to a caulking gun, is laying behind them. Isaac steps back in my view and he's holding a piece of black silk in his hand. My mind begins to race in anticipation.

"I want you to experience the sensation of our play tonight, Peaches. I don't want your vision to manipulate your mind, altering the sensations. So I'm going to blindfold you."

I nod in understanding because I can't find the words to express verbally. My world goes dark as the silk rests over my eyes.

"Remember, you have your safeword, baby." He breathes across my lips. I nod once again in acknowledgement.

Coolness flows over my face and I know Isaac has stepped away. His hand brushes over my plump mound and I hear subtle intake of breath.

"Your bare pussy pleases me. Considering your aversion to it during previous conversations, I'm surprised. Though pleasantly."

I can't help smiling, as he continues grazing his fingertips across my mons.

"What changed your mind?"

His question stuns me for a moment. *Why does he care, so long as I did it? Duh...I did it to please you. Silly man...*

"To please you, Master," I murmur softly.

I hate not being able to see his face. I understand him more through his expressions; a snippet of his true feelings.

Something placed on the areola of my right breast grabs my attention. It's moving around a bit. I assume he's moving it. It's cold...definitely glass. It stills and I hear a swooshing sound, like a pump. Simultaneously, my nipple is being sucked. Not by Isaac's mouth...it must be the bell shaped thingy. The suction increases. I inhale a short breath through my teeth, almost wincing. The suction stops increasing, but the pressure remains. I feel the familiar cold on my left breast and the process repeats.

The feeling is a little overwhelming. Sucking on my nipples is normally followed by tender lips and tongue caressing them. I want his lips on my nipples. They need caressing. I want these damn things off.

I feel his breath on my chest, his tongue circling the outer area of my breast, around whatever has my nipples under siege. I jerk my hands to no avail, desperately wanting his tongue to sooth my tender nipples. He smacks my outer left thigh.

"Be still Peaches. Savor the sensation, don't fight it. Slow, deep breaths, baby."

A small growl escapes my lips in frustration. *How long is he going to leave these fucking things on???* I take a deep breath like he said, letting it out slowly. I repeat this a few times, slowing my breathing, calming down; while he teases my breasts.

My calm is disrupted and panic ensues, when the cool sensation surrounds my clit. *Oh HELL NO!!!*

"NO...please! I'm begging Master," I plea.

"Sub, I know you're not telling your Master what to do," he scolds.

"I can hardly stand them on my nipples, Master. I will surely die with it on my clit." *God, I hate not being able to see his face!*

A roar of laughter thunders from his chest, as I feel him

spread my folds and adjust the glass torture bell.

"Baby, when I'm finished with you tonight, you'll be begging me to do this again," he chuckles. Somehow I don't quite believe him.

The pressure building around my clit instantly changes my mind. It's building slower around my sex than it did on my nipples, but the sensation has me squirming near the edge of ecstasy. *Oh my God!!!*

I whimper, as his tongue divides the folds of my sex, nibbling and tugging along the way. A tremor unfurls throughout my body as my clit throbs with every beat of my heart. The pressure ceases its escalation, its grip firmly in place. My body is trembling with the need to release.

"I can't take it anymore, Master. I need to come...PLEASE!"

"Not yet, baby. I want you to see my handy work. It's amazing!" He says with such adoration and almost instantly the blindfold is removed.

Blinking several times, it takes a moment for my eyes to adjust to the light. Refocused, my eyes travel down to my breast. I gasp in astonishment at the contraption on the end of each breast. Isaac takes hold of the device.

He looks delectable. Broad, muscular, bare chest and torso; hulking arms; and ruggedly sexy face. My eyes rove to the top of his leather pants, open with the fat head of his cock exposed to me. There's not a twenty or thirty-year-old, that has anything on this strappin' sexy man. *What does he see in me???*

"Take a deep breath, it'll be a little painful when the blood rushes back," he advises as he pushes the valve to release the pressure.

I hiss at the release, but the ache is alleviated by the tenderness of Isaac's lips. He alternates between each nipple, giving me what I've been craving. I'm mesmerized by the size of my nipples. They're enormous and so erogenous. Each flick of his tongue sends a jolt straight to my entrapped clit, which drives my need even higher. I moan my need for more. *Yes...I want more. More pressure...release. More pressure. Fuck...I don't know what I want.*

My fists clench and struggle futilely. Isaac reads my body and increases the pressure around my clit. Tears are pooling in my eyes, but the pain feels so good I don't want it to stop.

Within seconds, the pressure dissipates and I wail my displeasure. *I begged him not to do it, now I'm protesting its removal.*

"So fucking beautiful, baby. An enormous pink pearl!" He gasps in awe.

I catch a glimpse and my eyes widen in amazement. My clit's protruding passed my folds and it's ultra-sensitive. I'll come if he breathes on it.

On that thought, he devours my clit; sucking and lavishing it with his wicked oral skills. I'm writhing with need; whimpering with every delicious flick of his tongue.

"PLEASE Master...please."

"You're so wet for me, Peaches. You taste so sweet."

"I'm begging...," I sob.

"Who's in control, Peaches?"

"M-master is in control," I whine.

"Good girl."

"Do you need to be fucked, baby?" He moans in my mouth.

"YES...," I breathe.

With that, Isaac grabs my hips dragging my ass to the

edge and impales me with one swift thrust of his massive cock.

"OH MY GOD!!!!" I scream, beads of sweat dotting my forehead.

He's pounding unrelentingly and each stroke grinds across my engorge clit, igniting it like a flint to a stone.

My body is trembling with a fury that needs releasing. Knowing my body, Sir unleashes me.

"COME NOW!" He roars with his own release.

And I soar.

Chapter 17

Isaac

She took her punishment well. Better than I thought she would. She actually thought I'd forgotten, like I would forget a chance to redden her ass, not a chance. Anticipation is a form of punishment itself. Making her wait until Sunday was a good lesson for her.

She needed to experience true punishment and the stockade was the best thing. But I wanted it to be private, so waiting til the club was closed on Sunday would allow me that. I really wanted her lily white ass over my knee, but she likes spankings too much for it to be a punishment, plus I would've fucked her much sooner. Warming her up with my hand, relaxed her a bit, but it was very impersonal in the stocks. The flogger heated her up, and the quirt added some nice striped designs. I think I quelled her desire to degrade herself for a while.

Driving allows for too much thinking time. I typically take advantage of the quiet time to solve work problems, work out designs. But all I can think about is her going out of town today with that prick. Then Patrick telling me about the case he's working on; all the home invasions, women getting attacked.

Giving Katherine a crash course in self-defense last night; a few maneuvers to protect herself, was beneficial for her and quite pleasing to me. She's a feisty little minx; tough as nails. She can definitely give as good as she gets. If someone ever messed with her, they would have their hands full with that little hellcat. Her bite mark on my arm, from our training last night, has a bluish hue. The reminder puts a smile on my face and stiffness in my cock, remembering the fucking that followed.

It made sense to teach her self-defense in her home; utilizing what she has in her house to protect herself. I frankly enjoyed fucking her in her bed; but waking up in her bed this morning was not my intention. I've never stayed the night in a woman's bed, but I couldn't tear myself away from her. I didn't want to. *I'm in deep shit...*

****

Damn I'm sore. The flight to Chicago, sitting in meetings all day, and of course my rock'em sock'em training with Isaac last night. I haven't wrestled around like that since I was a teenager fighting with my brothers. But wrestling with Isaac has delicious benefits. He was hell bent on teaching me to bring a man to his knees, mercilessly. The memory has my sex quivering.

I still can't believe that Isaac spent the night. His wake-up alarm is simply… A-mazing! A girl could get used to that.

"Dinner…7:30 at Sweetwater on Michigan Avenue. Is that good for everybody?" Someone in the conference room calls out, interrupting my thoughts.

I nod in agreement, packing my things back in my briefcase. It's already 5:30 and I haven't checked into the hotel yet. We came to the meeting straight from the airport. I retrieve my overnight bag from the closet in the conference room. Rushing out of the office, I didn't want to get caught up walking with Rick. I quickly make my way down the block to the hotel.

The view of Lake Michigan is breathtaking. The suite is half the size of my house. A beautiful silvery gray sectional sofa with glass tables; with deep orchid accents. It's absolutely stunning.

Other than a text, as requested, letting him know I arrived safely; I haven't had a chance to check in with Isaac all day. We worked through lunch. I check my phone and have 2 missed calls; from Matt and Isaac. I check my voicemail; Matt's working this weekend, so he's not coming home. *I hate he didn't come home from college for the summer, but he's got a good job and he doesn't want to risk losing it for the fall. My baby boy is all grown. Ben leaves for France in a couple weeks, so neither will be home much this summer. They're finding their way in the world. Crazy how time flies.*

Second message is from Isaac... "Just checking in." I hit the 'call back' button.

"Hey, Baby... busy day?" His sultry voice coats my ear.

"Very. Sorry I didn't get a chance to call before now; we worked through lunch."

"No worries. Any problems? Has the prick been minding his manners?" He snarks, not even trying to hide his disdain.

"No issues. Actually, I've had no interaction with Rick, at all. We sat on opposite ends of the plane and opposite ends of the huge conference table."

"GOOD!" He snaps in reply.

"How was your day, Sir?" I sweeten my tone in effort to calm him.

"Busy. They have a clusterfuck here. The building is for a family business, a large family, and no one can agree on anything. They've been driving my foreman insane changing their minds every time the wind changes direction. I'm putting a stop to that shit today," he grouses.

"I'm sorry you're having a shitty...I mean bad day, Sir." I quickly correct myself. *He can cuss all he wants, but I can't. Double standard...*

"Good save, Peaches," he chuckles.

"My day got a helluva lot better, hearing your voice," his tone dropping an octave; warm and decadent.

"I hate to cut our talk short Sir, but I have a client dinner to attend in less than an hour and I still need to shower," I mumble with a hint of disappointment. *Our previous talks have led to very interesting activities.*

"I understand, baby. Call me when you get back to your room. Be good and be safe."

"Yes, Sir."

****

This restaurant is phenomenal. The food was presented so elegantly, I didn't want to eat. However, I did and it was exquisite. Several people wanted to go dancing, so we head to the club next door.

The music is thumpin' and the women head to the dance floor, shakin' our ass for a while. Dying of thirst, I head to the bar for a bottle water. I 'm not a big drinker anyways, but I never consume alcohol on business trips. It's afterhours, but I still feel I'm representing my company. Unfortunately, Rick doesn't seem to share the same thought.

He had several drinks at dinner and is tossing them back one after another, here. His philandering behaviors have kicked into high gear. He's literally groping an ad rep that works for our client. The woman has the very familiar look of disgust plastered on her face; the one Rick tends to ignite in women.

SHIT... he's going to ruin this deal if he doesn't stop. Others from the group have noticed.

"Katherine, what the hell is up with Rick?" Nancy, one of the vendor reps, asks in disbelief.

"I don't know, Nancy. I've never seen him quite like

this," I reply honestly. Because I've never seen him this blatant. He's usually a little more subtle.

"Well... you know, Mr. Douglas, VP of Syntec, right?" She asks.

"Of course...He's making the final decision on our presentation," I remark nervously.

"Well... the girl Rick has his hands all over is Mr. Douglas' sex-a-tary," she blurts out.

"Un-fucking-believable!"

Without thinking, I storm over to the bar where Rick is ordering yet another drink. Though this allows the girl to escape his pilferage of her body.

"What are you doing? Do you know who that woman is that you're groping?" I hiss through clenched teeth.

"What...am I doing? He slurs as he tries to focus his glassy eyes.

"You're gonna cost us this account? We've all worked too hard on this account for you to screw it up. Now, get your shit together, Rick. Drink water!"

Out of the corner of my eye, I see Mr. Douglas heading

our way, with his sex-a-tary, all up in his ear. *Oh, shit... what am I gonna do?*

"Katherine, I know how much time and energy you put into your presentation, so I'm extending some lenience, but you need to get that drunk fuck out of here, NOW!" Mr. Douglas snarls, red faced and brimming with anger.

"Yes, S - Mr. Douglas." *Nope, not sir. You are not my Sir.*

I think it's a little ironic how one married man is fuming with anger because another married man was groping a woman he's sleeping with, but neither man is married to. I shake my head, rolling my eyes.

I grab Rick by the arm pulling him outside. The hotel's just a couple of blocks away. I'm hoping the cool breeze from Lake Michigan will sober him up, he's staggering all over the place. If it weren't for the millions of dollars this presentation means for our company, I'd leave his ass on the street.

Finally, at the hotel, this drunk ass doesn't even remember his room number. I stop at the desk and get Rick's room number. He fumbled in his pockets and finally found the key card for his room, not before bouncing his head off the side of the elevator when he lost his balance.

"I know you want me, Kat," Rick slurs as he's swaying back and forth in the elevator.

"Don't be absurd," I bark cutting him with my eyes.

"You do...I know it," he giggles like an obnoxious school girl.

"Just shut up, Rick"

Finally the elevator stops on the 25th floor. *That took forever.* Wobbling to and fro, we make it to his door. He leans against the wall while I try to open the door. His arms wrap around mine from behind; the stench of alcohol and smoke laced breath besiege my nose.

"What are you doing? MOVE!" I growl ramming my elbow back.

The door opens and I turn to leave, when I'm shoved against the door. My heart begins to pound in my chest. *What the fuck is he doing?!?!*

"I know you want me, Kat. You just play hard to get," He boasts as he grips the front of my blouse.

"I know you're drunk Rick, but you need to stop. And stop... NOW!" I grit, trying to push him away. He's not a very big man, nowhere the size of Isaac, but he's still pretty strong.

"I know you're jealous of that pretty bitch tonight, but don't worry Kat, there's enough of me to go around." He slurs, as the stench besieging my nose, inundates my mouth as he presses his mouth to mine.

Fury erupts and my hand instantly burns from the blow I land to the side of Rick's face, breaking his grip on me.

"Get the FUCK away! I rage and storm off.

I'm still shaking with anger when I get to my room. *I'm gonna kick his ass. He has crossed the line. Drunk or not, he's crossed the line...No excuse!*

Standing beneath the steaming hot water, I scrub every inch of my body. I nearly drown myself running water up my nose to wash that nasty smell away. *What the fuck is wrong with him? This shit has to stop.*

I pull on Isaac's t-shirt, the one he wore last night. It still holds his musky scent. Its effects on me better than any glass of wine, shot of whiskey, or prescription pill; at calming my nerves. *I wonder if he realizes I took it. I snicker to myself.*

Before I call him, I debate on whether to tell Isaac over the phone about the incident with Rick, or wait until we're face to face. He's held such contempt for Rick because of the incidences at work that I've shared with him. I can't imagine how he will react when I tell him about Rick's drunken behavior tonight.

I garner more from Isaac's expressions than I do his words, so I believe waiting will be best. And honestly, I've had enough emotional turmoil for one night. I grab my phone to call him...

"Hey baby...," He answers in his sleepy, gravelly voice. *Ooops, I woke him up.*

"You back in your room?" More a statement than question.

"Yes, Sir. I'm sorry I woke you. I shouldn't have called so late," I apologize with sincerity.

"If you hadn't called, I'd blister your backside, being that I told you to call," he threatens with that voice that has my sex pulsing.

"Promises, promises...," I tease.

"Keep it up, mouthy wench. I'll stripe that ass some more when you get home."

I heard him stretch and yawn. And as contagious as

they are, I yawn, too.

"I know you've had a long day, Peaches. Get some sleep and I'll talk to you in the morning."

Great...no questions about Rick!

"Oh, how was dinner?"

DAMN....

"Dinner was wonderful," I beam when enthusiasm.

He only asked about dinner. And dinner was great.

"Good to hear. Get some rest... I'll talk to you tomorrow."

"Okay. Good night..."

"Oh, and Peaches... Read all you want tonight, but remember your orgasms belong to me," he chuckles wickedly.

Smartass....

Chapter 18

My morning video *chat* with Isaac was just the stress reliever I needed after last night. I would never have dreamed of having video sex before, now Isaac has spoiled me, especially when we're apart. He thought he was being cute last night, insinuating I would masturbate reading my book. Little does he know after a fucking from him, he's ruined me for other men and books. Now, to face the shitty day that lays before me.

God, I dread the presentation this morning; standing beside the man I slapped the shit out of, just a few hours ago. If that's not bad enough, the man who's fuck-toy the aforementioned "slapped man" was groping only a short time before that, will be sitting at the end of the conference table determining the fate of our presentation. I feel like I'm walking into a mine field. I lean against the back of the elevator for the long decent to the lobby, trying to determine how to salvage this deal.

The elevator makes several stops and I'm so lost in my

misery that I didn't realize Rick had entered the elevator and was standing beside me.

"Nice right hook you have," he says with a forced snicker.

"I slapped you. I didn't punch you," I curtly reply, facing forward, avoiding eye contact.

"You split my lip..."

"Good! Pull that shit again, your lip won't be the only thing split," I threaten with venom.

"Look, I'm sorry. I was drunk and got a little carried away," he sighed. If there was an ounce of remorse in his statement, I didn't hear it.

"*A little carried away* – so that's what you call it," I snark. Thankfully the elevator's not crowded, but I really don't care who hears.

"I hope you have a plan to salvage this deal."

"What do you mean?" He asks turning toward me.

This project is doomed and this buffoon doesn't have a clue to the havoc he caused last night. *What a dumbass!*

"The woman you had your hands all over last night is

the secretary of Mr. Douglas...you know, VP of Syntec. And by secretary...I mean secretary with special benefits."

"FUCK!!!" He groans, wrenching his hands through his hair.

So much for drawing attention to us, as the elderly woman in front of us turns and glares at Rick.

"Yeah...fun times await us," I sneer, rolling my eyes.

Stepping off the elevator, I turn toward Rick. I notice a bluish hue on the left side of his face near his mouth, close to the puffiness on his lip.

"I'll meet you there. I need to make a stop on my way." I call out turning toward the coffee shop. *I wonder if they can put a double shot of Bailey's in the java for me.*

****

Presentation's over, but Mr. Douglas asked us to wait for his decision. *That's a bad sign. Most clients take days, if not weeks to make a decision, and he's making his moments after the presentation. Not good...*

We're sitting just outside the conference room, similar

to sitting outside the principal's office in school. The walls are glass, so we can see the discussions going on, except Mr. Douglas; I can't see him. They have the pleasure of watching Rick and I squirm waiting on their decision. Rick hasn't uttered a word since the presentation. I have to hand it to him...if he was nervous, he didn't show it. He went right through the presentation with such self-assuredness; almost like last night never happened.

The click of the door opening startles me, as I didn't see anyone get up. Mr. Douglas approaches us, Rick and I stand.

"I've known your boss, Rob, for many years. We've done business together years ago," Mr. Douglas begins, almost mid thought. "After last night, friend or not, I had no intention of doing any more business with Atlanta Media."

I nod in understanding, not knowing what else to do, since the floor is not opening up to swallow me whole, saving me from this embarrassment. Mr. Douglas appears to be talking directly to me. His eyes have not shifted toward Rick, yet. A feat which appears deliberate.

"However, your presentation was flawless, Katherine. And in business, I have to set aside emotions and personal feelings to make the best business decisions. So I am accepting your offer, with a few stipulations that I'll discuss personally with Rob; foremost being a new sales rep. I know you're not the sales rep, Katherine, but you sold this one. Maybe a shift away from crunching numbers is in your future," Mr. Douglas chuckles, paying no regard to Rick.

I offer my hand to shake with Mr. Douglas. "Thank you for your kind words, Mr. Douglas, but I think I need to stick with the numbers," I smile.

Rick offers his hand to Mr. Douglas, "Thank..."

"Your ass would be fired, if you were my employee," Mr. Douglas growls, knocking Rick's offered hand away. "You almost cost your employer a multimillion dollar deal, you piece of shit. I can't fire you, but I will make damn sure you have nothing to do with this account," he sneers at Rick.

"I look forward to working with you, Katherine," he calls back as he's walking away.

****

Thankfully, once again, Rick and I were on opposite ends of the plane on the flight home. I still can't believe how irresponsible Rick's behavior was, on a business trip no less. I sling my travel bag over my shoulder and head to my car.

Traffic is a nightmare around the airport with all this construction; but when hasn't there been construction at the Atlanta Airport? Or traffic for that matter?

Creeping along the highway, it dawns on me that I haven't turned my phone back on from the flight. Powered up, it immediately beeps a message.

ISAAC: Not gonna make it home tonight. Are you back, yet?

ME: Yes...just left the airport.

ISAAC: Ok...Can you open the club? If not, I'll call Derek. Pat's tied up at work.

ME: I'm stuck in traffic, but I'll try to get there in time. I'll call Derek, if I can't.

ISAAC: Good Girl! Gotta run...I'll call you later tonight.

ME: Yes, Sir. :)

No time to go home, so I head straight to Nexus. I'm a tad late, but the cleaning company waited for me. I make the rounds checking supply stock in theme rooms and the stations around the club. I linger in the medical room, reminiscing about my last visit in here. My clit begins to throb just thinking about it. *Cupping – the deviant little bell shapes that sucked my nipples and clit to gargantuan size. Damn...* Let me get out of here before I get in trouble.

By the time I make it back to the lobby, the staff is here and a few members are trickling through the door. After an extended session of chit-chatting with Gina, Tiny, and Zeke; I head to the office to hunker down to work.

Before I know it, a couple hours have passed. I'm starving...gurgling sounds are echoing through my body. I'm so hungry my stomach is gnawing on my spine. Hopefully Derek will be here soon. He called earlier to see if anybody needed anything because he was stopping to pick up dinner. It was then I realized I hadn't had anything to eat all day.

"Food's here," Derek calls out, standing at the office door. "I'm gonna eat at the bar. Do you want to join me?" He offers.

My growling stomach must have summoned him. "Sure...let me wrap this up and I'll be right over."

Dinner was delish and so was the company. Derek is caramel dipped sex on a stick. I can't believe he's not married and not in a relationship. SINGLE... *what the hell!* He's known Isaac for a long time. Interesting to find out that he was Isaac's attorney for his divorce, just out of law school; before his days as a prosecutor in the DA's office.

Rounding the corner toward the office, I hear a familiar shrill voice. I stop just short of rounding the wall, out of their view. Listening carefully, my heart thunders in my chest at the realization of who's talking to Gina...

"Yeah...I know my master is out of town. I was with him last night, but I needed to come back in town today to handle some business," the deception rolling easily off the tongue of that conniving bitch.

I step from behind the wall, my suspicion confirmed.

"Can I help you...Vickie, isn't it?" I quip.

She turns on her heels to face me. "No, I don't think so...Master Isaac took care of me last night," she sneers with a smirk.

My blood is searing with fury, spreading like wildfire through my veins. I clinch my fists to calm the rage trembling in them. Knowing good and damn well, she wasn't with him.

"Get out. You lying piece of shit...Get the FUCK OUT!!!"

I roar, not giving a shit who hears.

Tiny has her by the arm, hauling her out the door, while Gina stares, mouth gaping at me like I've grown ten heads.

Making no response, I take a couple cleansing breaths, then walk into the office, slamming the door behind me.

Stupid bitch...stupid, stupid bitch. Though I'm not sure who's more stupid; Vickie or me. I should never have exploded like that. This is a business, after all. I should have controlled my temper better than that.

I bury myself in work until closing time. Opening the door, I notice most of the staff gathered at the counter, in a hushed conversation. Hesitantly, I step closer to them and the talking stops, as their stares burn into me.

"I'm terribly sorry for my outburst earlier tonight. There's no excuse for it. I hope you all will forgive me. Were there any complaints from members?" I nervously ramble.

Their silence was deafening before being shattered by Tiny. "Damn, I was hoping to see a beat down. That bitch has an ass whoppin' coming her way and I just knew you were gonna deliver it, Kat," he booms and they all break out in laughter.

"And no...members weren't aware of anything," Derek continues grinning ear to ear.

"Thank goodness!" I sigh in relief. "Tiny...I'll keep your beat down in mind," I giggle. "Let's go home."

We all head to the parking area. Approaching my car, I notice it slightly leaning. I can't really see anything for certain, even though the area is well lit. I walk around to the passenger side and see the rear tire is flat.

"SHIT..."

Chapter 19

"Hey babe...are you already home?" Isaac asks answering his phone.

"I'm afraid not. I'm still at Nexus...I have a flat tire," I grumble into the phone.

"A flat tire?"

"Yeah, I must've ran over something. There was a lot of construction around the airport this evening. We were leaving and when I walked toward my car, I noticed it was leaning," I explain.

"Are you alone?"

"No, Derek's here with me. He came back in to wait with me while I call a tow truck."

"You're not calling a tow truck this time of night. You don't know who will come out there. Could be some sick fuck that will have all your information and know where you live," Isaac growls. "Stay at my place. You have the code and the spare key is in my desk. The truck and Camaro are both there.

Drive either one of them tomorrow. I'll call a buddy first thing in the morning to come get your car and get the tire changed."

"Hmmm…the Camaro, huh. I'd like to take that sweet thing for a test ride," I chuckle.

"Have at it, Peaches," he offers is a challenge like manner.

"Your '69 Camaro???" I shrill. "You must be crazy? My luck, the sky really would fall…right on top of that black beauty. And my ass couldn't take the pummeling you would give it. The F150 will do just fine."

Laughter roars in my ear. "Suit yourself."

Thank goodness he can't see my eye-rolling…he's not too fond of that particular habit of mine.

"Are you sure you want me to stay at your place?" I ask sheepishly.

"I wouldn't have told you to, if I didn't," he remarks.

"Well…Okay, if you're sure."

"Katherine…," He growls, his voice dropping an octave.

"Sorry, Sir," I croon. I do need to let Derek know he doesn't need to stick around."

"Fine...call me when you get settled upstairs."

"Yes, Sir."

Derek offers to get my travel bag from my car. He's such a great guy; so polite. Guess it's a good thing I didn't have time to go home before coming here or I wouldn't have a change of clothes for work tomorrow. I always pack extra clothes when traveling; you never know what's gonna happen. I try to be prepared for anything; very much a realist and I don't like surprises.

Locking the door behind Derek and Isaac's spare key in hand, I head upstairs.

****

I feel like an intruder being in Isaac's home without him here. Isaac is protective of his privacy, so allowing me to stay here without him makes my mind race with possibilities. Trying not to read too much into it, I can't stop the fluttering in my heart.

His home is quite unique. He told me it was once a twenty-two room plantation house; including 12 bedrooms. He completely renovated the home; building Nexus downstairs and a private residence for him upstairs. Downstairs, Nexus has an open play dungeon, a bar, dance floor, private theme rooms, and a separate locker room for men and women. Upstairs, he knocked down several walls to provide a living and entertainment room, kitchen, and dining area. One room remains as a guest bedroom, while another has been adapted to a mini-dungeon, including a St. Andrew's Cross.

When touring his home for the first time, I inquired to his need for a playroom in his residence, if he didn't bring women upstairs. He replied he'd always had a playroom of some type, so when he was remodeling, he included it in the plans. He also said it was never his intention not to bring women to the residence, he just fell into the pattern and discovered he enjoyed his privacy. That night, he said he used it for target practice with his whip. However, my ass has been blistered several times on that cross since that first night. The thought makes my sex twitch.

I toss my bag on his bed. His bedroom is suited for a *Master*. A king size, solid oak bed is the centerpiece in this enormous room. Though it's the size of two bedrooms, it's warm and cozy with neutral colors of black, gray, slate and taupe. A blend of sleek, elegant, and ruggedness...a gentleman.

Desperate for a shower...in his shower, I quickly

undress. Stepping into the "walk-in closet" that is his shower, I'm pelted in multiple directions by streams of water in varying intensity. The shower head's the size of a large platter, raining down steam, washing away my day. It feels like being in a carwash, but for your body. It's pure heaven!

The shirt Isaac wore to dinner Monday night, is laying across the chair beside his bed. *Yep...that's what I'm wearing to bed.* Buttoning the shirt in the middle, I climb in the middle of his bed to give him a call.

"Hey babe. You settled in?" His gravelly voice answers the phone.

"Yes, Sir. Thank you for letting me stay here tonight."

"My pleasure...well mostly, anyway. Thoughts of you in my bed make my cock throb. But seeing as I'm not there...I'm not too happy about that," he grouses. "What are you gonna do about that, Peaches?"

"U-ummm...what would you like me to do?"

"Get your laptop?" He growls.

"Oh...ok." *Mmmm...video "chat" time.*

Laptop chatting is much better than chatting by the phone. The phone can be a little herky jerky sometimes. The laptop has a very minimal delay.

Shit...his delicious cock is in full view; it's thick head glistening like dew at the tip.

"Lean back against the headboard...spread your legs," he commands. His cock still in view.

I adjust the laptop between my legs, glancing over at the small box on the screen to check out his view. *Damn...I shouldn't have looked. My ass needs a wide load sign.*

"Let me see my pussy... spread those lips."

My heart begins to flutter as I do what I'm told, spreading my folds for him.

"Ok, baby...your hands are now mine. I wanna see if my pussy's wet."

I slowly drag my finger between my folds, inserting the tip of my finger in my opening.

"That's it baby...now deeper. I want to feel the silken walls of my pussy."

My finger glides through the slicken opening, deep in my sex.

"Slide my wet finger across my fat clit. Round and

round, baby."

Inhaling a slight gasp, I circle my clit; wanting to grind into my hand.

"I wanna see my luscious tits."

Grinding into my fingertip, I open my shirt...his shirt; exposing my breasts to him. Closing my eyes, finding a delicious rhythm.

"Mmmm...I love your tits, baby. They're fucking beautiful. Put my hands where you want them," he moans softly.

The sound of his voice draws my eyes to the laptop; his hand stroking his cock in fluid motion. An erotic surge overcomes me. I want to feel him, taste him.

Grating into my palm, I grip my left nipple; pinching and pulling. I release my grip, circling the elongated nub softly. Then gripping my nipple again, I repeat the process again and again, my hips grinding rhythmically.

"Damn...baby. I need to be balls deep in my pussy," he gasps breathlessly.

"I need to come...," I cry out.

"Come now, baby."

I catch a glimpse of his assault on his cock and it catapults me into a deliriously erotic state.

Nipples hardened like pebbles, I grasp my left breast, forcefully pulling it upward. My tongue flicks across the sensitive nub, circling it round and round. I faintly hear groans, penetrating my thoughts, surging me higher.

I flick my tongue across the nub once again, before wrapping my lips around the pink pebble, lavishing it with my tongue and latching it between my teeth; wishing it was Isaac.

A roar shatters the silence, as I witness Isaac's eruption... just as I find my own release.

****

I startle awake when the beeping sounds from my phone. Blinking several times to clear the confusion, I try to focus on my surroundings. *Hmmm...not my bed.* Realization quickly dawns, remembering where I am and why. Snuggled in his pillow, I smell him and I bury my face deeper in the softness. I could lay here all day, wrapped in his musky scent.

I force myself out of bed and have another, quicker

round in his luxurious shower. Tidying up, I gather my things, leaving his home the way I found it. Though that beautiful Camaro is tempting to drive...I make the wise choice to drive the truck.

It's not the Camaro, but his truck is none too shabby either. Definitely not his work truck. A black Ford F150 Super Cab, black on black. Much bigger than my Honda, I park near the back of the lot to give myself a little extra room to maneuver.

I notice Rick smoking outside when I approach the building. Staring at me, I throw up my hand and offer a "Good Morning." He makes no response as I enter the building. I'm sure he will have his head handed to him on a platter once Mr. Douglas talks to Rob about the incident in Chicago.

Swamped with work, the morning flies by. I meet Deb for lunch and share all the gory details about my trip, my flat tire, and staying at Isaac's last night.

"You really need to watch yourself around that jerk, Kathy. He seems a little unstable," Deb warns with furrowed brows.

"He's just irresponsible, especially when he drinks too much."

“So, what did Isaac say about it all?”

“I haven’t told him, yet”

“Oh, Kathy…you need to tell him.”

“I am. I just didn’t want to tell him over the phone. I’m gonna talk to him tonight, hopefully. If he gets back in town.”

Anxious from our talk at lunch, I head to my desk to bury myself in work. Just settled in, Rob calls me into his office. Dreading this conversation, I trudge to his office.

Fortunately for me, Mr. Douglas has filled Rob in on all the sordid details. Rob just wanted to confirm what I witnessed. Wrestling whether or not to tell Rob about the incident between Rick and me, it appears Rick will be in enough trouble with the Mr. Douglas issues, so I keep it to myself.

Needing to get out of here on time today, I hunker down with work to get caught up with other accounts, neglected while I was away in Chicago. I’m meeting Ben after work to pick up his suits for his trip to France and then we’re having dinner. I’m looking forward to it. Both of the boys have been so busy with work and school, I haven’t seen them much.

Patrick is going to open Nexus if Isaac doesn’t get back

in town in time. I haven't seen Patrick much lately, either. He's working on some big case that's keeping him very busy. I probably should text Isaac to remind him I'll be late for work tonight.

ME: Just a reminder, I'll be late tonight. Errands & dinner with Ben.

ISAAC: Got it covered. By the way...my buddy called, said you didn't run over a nail. Said your tire was slashed! WTF???

ME: WHAT?!?!? Are you Serious?!?!

ISAAC: He said you must've pissed somebody off.

ME: No...there has to be some kind of mistake. I haven't pissed nobody off enough to do that. *Or have I???*

ISAAC: We'll talk tonight...

ME: Ok...be safe.

My stomach lodges in my throat. There has to be some kind of mistake. Who would want to slash my tires???

****

Isaac

The electrician finally got his head out of his ass and the problem solved. I hate traveling and I need to be home. The thoughts of somebody being malicious enough to slash Katherine's tire, makes my skin crawl. I'm gonna talk to Patrick and get to the bottom of this.

Damn…that girl tore my nerves up last night. Laying in my bed, fingering herself was torture enough, but sucking and biting her own nipple, sent me over the fucking edge. It was all I could do, to keep the beast within, locked away. We will be talking about that.

Pulling into the driveway, I see Katherine's car parked where my truck usually sits, so she's not here yet.

I head to my office, which is honestly Katherine's. She's in here working more than me. I wade through a stack of mail, waiting for her to get here.

The clicking sound of the door draws my attention to it, knowing it's Katherine.

"Hey babe," I announce, stunned into silence at the sight.

"Master....," grates through my ears.

Slamming my chair against the wall, I stalk around to the front of the desk.

"WHAT THE FUCK ARE YOU DOING HERE???" I explode across the room.

"M-master, I didn't know you were here."

That voice making my skin crawl.

"I'm not your fucking master, Vickie. Why are you here?"

"I umm, I...came to see..." She stammers along.

"Cut the shit, Vickie. You've been told to stay away."

"I umm, lost my bracelet last night when Tiny threw me out."

"Last night...you were here last night?" I ask puzzled.

"Yeah, 'til that bitch office worker threw a hissy fit and kicked me out."

Vickie crosses the floor toward me, wrapping her arms around my neck. Her touch feels like acid on my skin.

"I've missed you Master," she croons trying to kiss me.

Grabbing her arms from around my neck, I shove her back. Staggering a bit, she catches herself and slithers back in front of me.

“I need your touch, Master. I need your pain,” she whispers in my ear.

“You need to leave...NOW! And don’t come back!” I bark, pushing her away again.

“I know that fat bitch don’t do anything for you. I know what you need. Let me give you what you need, Master,” she moans, dropping to her knees, grasping my cock in her hand.

My cock even knows she’s a disease, eating away at everything she touches; it doesn’t even flinch. Flaccid.

As I grab her shoulders to pull her to her feet, the office door opens...

“Well, Hey, S-...,” the cheerful greeting abruptly cut short.

A myriad of emotions flash across Katherine’s face, my mind trying to decipher everyone. Simultaneously, the bitch buries her face in my crotch.

“Katherine, it’s not wh-,” I try to explain, as she stomps out, slamming the door behind her.

Violently shoving Vickie to the floor, I storm toward the door after her.

"Katherine...STOP!" I blast across the lobby.

Stopping...she turns back toward me, rage rolling from her soul.

"Fuck you, Isaac! FUCK YOU!!!"

Chapter 20

My heart's pounding out of my chest, I'm desperately searching for my car. Panning the lot...I don't see it AND I don't have my keys.

"GRRRRRR... what the hell am I gonna do?" I yell at the stars, tears streaking my face.

Hearing commotion behind me, I bolt to the only thing I have a key to; Isaac's truck. No time to worry about my car...I gotta get away from here.

Rubber gripping the pavement and the bed of the truck so light; I fishtail slightly when I slam the pedal to the floor. I barely make out the image of Isaac standing at the edge of the driveway, through the blur of tears, as I roar by. *Asshole...*

I am so stupid. What the hell was I thinking getting involved in this...this life; involved with him. I should've known better. He told me it was training; told me he didn't have relationships. But I wouldn't listen...nope not me. I read too much into everything he said, everything he did; making something out of nothing. The way I always do. I shouldn't be mad at him. He did exactly what he said he would; train me, teach me about the lifestyle. Nope...this is all my fault. I fell for him...I'm the pathetic loser.

"Stupid, stupid, stupid!!!" I pound my fists on the steering wheel, wailing into the night.

His thundering ringtone is blowing up my phone. Feeling in my purse for my phone, the thundering vibrates once again. Grabbing hold of it, my wandering fingers end the call. Twenty-seven missed calls; six voice mails; four text messages; in less than 20 minutes. I power off the phone, as it roars again. I can't talk to him; I can't see him.

Locking the front door behind me, I can't get out of these clothes fast enough. It's like their toxic; the scratchy feel of humiliation and the pungent smell of abasement. I scour myself under steaming water, trying to wash the heartache from my soul. Downing a couple glasses of wine, I crawl in bed. Dragging the covers over my shoulders, I sink into my pillow in search of a restful night.

****

Sleep evades me all night, tossing and turning. Whenever I did close my eyes, visions of that bitch on her knees, hand gripping his cock, filled my head. A debate rages in my head; work...sick day, work...sick day??? I want to hide from the world and lick my wounds. If I stay home, I'll replay last night over and over in my head, making myself miserable. Nobody will know anything at work, I convince myself. That is if I can do something with these red swollen eyes. If anybody asks...it's allergies.

Heading out the door, it dawns on me that I still have Isaac's truck. I need to contemplate a plan to return his truck and get my car; all without seeing him.

Thankfully, the parking lot at work is empty, as is the lobby. Jean is busy with a phone call, so I throw up my hand in a wave and head to my desk.

The morning is slow, so it allows me time to think. *What am I gonna do about my job at the club? I really need it right now. Ben leaves for France next week and he's depending on me for financial help while he's there for school. This is too much all at once.*

I can be professional, again trying to assure myself. He made no commitment to me. Well...actually he did. He said we were to be monogamous during my training. Then what the fuck was he doing with that bitch??? Thoughts ramble through my mind.

Professional. He broke the training agreement, so our relationship will be strictly professional. Training came along after I was hired, it wasn't a job requirement. So I will work at NEXUS, but my training is over. My stomach rolls and I become nauseous at the thought of Isaac never touching me again. But I can do this; I have to do this. Ben needs me to do this. *However, Isaac may not want me to work there anymore.*

I know I'm not ready to talk to him or face him, but I need my car. I ponder a moment and then he hits me... "Ms. Glancey".

"Thank you for calling J & J Contractors, may I help you?" Answers the sweet, firm voice.

"Hi, could I leave a message for Mr. Jameson?" I meekly ask.

"Mr. Jameson is in, may I tell him who's calling?" Ms. Glancey curtly replies.

"Hi Ms. Glancey, this is Katherine. I don't want to bother him, so if you'll just let him know that I'm not feeling well and won't be in tonight," I say quickly.

"Well hello, Katherine. I'm sorry you're not feeling well. He's in his office dear, I know he won't mind if I put your call through," her voice softening.

"No...please don't disturb him," I blurt in a panic. *I do not want to talk to him.*

"If you insist, dear. Just as well, his line just lit up. I'm sorry I was a little snippy when I answered, Katherine. But someone's been calling periodically the past few weeks, asking for Mr. Jameson, then hanging up before he answers. If he's not here, they ask when he's returning or if he's out of town, but they don't leave a message. I think someone's wanting to know when he's here and when he's not," Mrs. Glancey explains worriedly.

"Huh, that is weird, Ms. Glancey. It may not be a bad idea to tell him. You never know these days," I offer.

"Well, I'll give him your message, Katherine. Hope you feel better soon."

"Thank you! It's nothing serious. Probably a twenty-four hour virus," I lie. "Talk to you soon."

That worked perfectly. I didn't have to talk to Isaac and I found out he's at his office right now.

Since we're slow and I have lots of comp time built up, I buzz Jean to let her know I'm taking the afternoon off. She informs me I have two messages; one from Mr. Jameson and one from Debra. *Why is Debra calling my work number? Isaac called work because I'm not answering my cellphone. Though I'm still surprised he called work.*

I check my cellphone and realize I never turned it back on after turning it off last night. Powering it up, it lights up with notifications. Forty-three missed calls, twelve voicemails, and seventeen texts. *Wow...he's persistent. Or pissed.*

Scrolling through them, most are from Isaac but several of each are from Deb. Most of hers are about meeting for lunch and why I'm not answering my messages. I'm not brave enough to listen to or read Isaac's. I shoot Deb a text and tell her I'm super busy and can't get away for lunch. *Another lie...I'm going to hell.* I grab my things and head to Isaac's house to get my car.

Hauling ass toward Isaac's, my heart and stomach are fluttering. I know he's at work at the construction company, but the anticipation of possibly seeing him and having a confrontation, have made me a bundle of nerves.

Turning in the driveway, my stomach is churning so much, I think I'm going to be sick. A white-knuckle grip on the steering wheel, my palms are sweaty, my mouth like cotton, and my heart is pounding. *I'll absolutely die if he's here.* I pull around into the private residence driveway. *Shit…no car!*

Where the hell is my car??? The only cars here are the Camaro and work truck. I notice something white on the window of the Camaro. Stepping down out of the truck, I walk toward the Camaro. Sure enough…there's a note:

YOU WILL HAVE TO SEE ME TO GET YOUR CAR!!!

What the hell!!! That's blackmail…plain and simple! I grab a pen out of my purse and scribble my reply – "*Asshole…*" Fuming, I climb back in the truck and head home.

My phone is on, but I've silenced the ringer. Periodically, I check it to see what I've missed. Isaac has curtailed his calls and messages, only a few since lunch; Deb has a couple, and the boys too.

After a lengthy conversation with Deb about the events from last night, I'm mentally exhausted. Soaking in a hot bath, my tension eases and I relax a bit. I replay our talk in my head.

I'm a bit surprised at her, "*give him the benefit of the doubt, a chance to explain*" attitude; considering infidelity was the cause of her marriage ending. She also strongly suggested a "girls night out", something we haven't had in a while. I was reluctant to the idea at first, but the more I think about it, the more I think I need it and deserve it.

My conversation with Ms. Glancey earlier today, has me a little puzzled, too. She said someone is calling, asking for Isaac, but hanging up before he answers. And if he's not there, asking whether or not he's in town and not leaving a message. It's very strange.

Settled in for the night, I decide to take advantage of a quiet Friday night at home and do a little reading before bed.

****

Isaac

"Asshole..." She thinks keeping her car is being an asshole, she don't have a fucking clue... yet. When she's begging for an orgasm that I won't let her have, begging me to fuck her tight pussy and I won't... she'll understand then, what an asshole really is.

She called out sick...sick my ass. She's just avoiding the inevitable. Not answering my calls or returning my messages. She's writing punishment checks her ass can't cash, but I'll fucking enjoy collecting her debt.

She's taunting the beast. There's a reason they tell you not to poke wild animals and Katherine's about to find out why. For now, it remains caged; locked away, like it has been for many years. I'm giving her space to calm down. There's no way Katherine could keep me away, if it was unleashed.

What a clusterfuck! Vickie, that fucking bitch, is the cause of this mess. I guess I should consider myself lucky that Patrick was here last night to keep me from killing her or I'd be in jail.

She's here and gets kicked out by Katherine, the same night Katherine's tire gets slashed. Then shows up the next night, not expecting to see me. That bitch is up to something. Hopefully I incited enough fear in her last night to deter her evil path.

Chapter 21

After a slightly more restful night last night, I'm more convinced that I desperately need a night out. I call Deb and she's ecstatic with my decision. Now, to figure out what to do about work tonight. A thought I need to ponder a bit. Meanwhile, I decide to pamper myself with a mani/pedi; which is long overdue.

Sitting in this wondrous massaging chair, I catch up on all the social media notifications on my phone. No calls from Isaac today. I'm a little surprised and if I'm honest, a little hurt. As if my mind summoned him, my phone chirps with a text.

ISAAC: Feeling better? I expect you at work tonight.

'I expect you at work'...huh. He's got nerve. But I need to work, need the money.

Me: Yes...I'll be at work.

ISAAC: Good.

I wish he could see me sticking my tongue out at the

phone. He's such an arrogant ass, sometimes.

So, I've told Isaac I'm working and told Deb we're having a girl's night, now to make it all work out. Technically, I can do my job at Nexus, anytime. I don't have to wait until tonight. I can go in later this afternoon, get the work done and get out of there with plenty of time to party. I'll text Gina to make sure she'll be there tonight, so I don't leave them shorthanded. Perfect!

****

After spending an hour picking my outfit for tonight, I'm almost ready to go. To keep from changing at Nexus or having to come back home after work, I chose something a tad conservative for Nexus, but pretty risqué for me to wear to a dance club. Having to wear revealing clothes to work at Nexus, has begun to erode at my walls of self-consciousness.

A purple and black corset, along with a black, mid-thigh skirt is the choice for tonight. I grab my black sheer sweater to put on when Deb and I go dancing.

****

Putting off a confrontation with Isaac as long as possible, I park the truck in the club lot and not the residence area. A delivery truck is parked in front and my stomach goes to my throat. Shit...*Isaac is in the club already.*

I slowly saunter around the delivery truck and see Patrick's truck parked on the side.

"Hey Katherine, what are you doing here so early?" Patrick asks as he steps from behind the delivery truck, smiling that super sexy smile.

"Hi...," I hesitantly murmur. *I don't know if he witnessed my hissy fit Thursday night or not.* "I decided to come in early to get my work finished. I want to make it an early night."

"Oh...big plans tonight?" He smirks with a raised eyebrow.

Shit...what does he know? Sounds like he's fishing for information.

"Umm, not really. Just getting together with a friend."

"Yellow dress?" His eyes dancing.

"Excuse me?"

“Yellow dress. She came to Open House with you.”

“Oooh...Debra. Uh, yeah...I’m meeting Debra,” I confirm.

Every hint of playfulness leaves Patrick’s face.

“Look, you ladies need to be careful while you’re out and about tonight. Be aware of your surroundings at all times,” Patrick pleads. “I haven’t been around the club much lately because I’m working a big case. I’m sure you’ve heard about the home invasions and sexual assaults on the news. I can’t tell you much, just be alert.”

I have heard about it on the news and the fact they have no leads or suspects. Isaac had told me Patrick was working a big case, keeping him busy.

“We will,” I assure him. A little shaken after my conversation with Patrick, I head inside to get busy.

Peace, quiet, and no interruptions allow me to work swiftly through the paperwork that piled up over the past two days. I check the clock and it’s almost 9pm. Debra’s meeting me here and she’ll be here any minute. I brought my spare key to my car, so I can get my car back, regardless. I heard Isaac’s voice outside the office door earlier, so I know he’s here, though he hasn’t come in the office. I tidy up and gather my things. I scribble a note letting Isaac know where to find the key to his truck. As I round the corner of the desk, the door opens and Isaac steps in.

A flutter begins in my tummy, quickly accelerating to full blown tremors throughout my body. He's just staring at me. His eyes are dark and penetrating my soul.

"Going somewhere?" Isaac hisses.

His glacial tone turns my nervousness to derision.

"Yep...," I snap back. "Can I get the key to my car? I left your truck key in the locked desk drawer."

"You said you were working tonight? What's going on?" He snarls back at me.

I'm not getting in a pissing match with him. I take a deep breath to calm down.

"I came in early today, to get caught up. I've got plans tonight, but I made sure Gina would be here so you wouldn't be in a bind."

"Plans...with???" He asks through clenched teeth.

This is getting nowhere, fast. I'll just ride with Deb and get my car later.

"Friends," I snark, brushing past him and out the door.

Of all nights for Deb to be running late. I storm out of the office like I'm going somewhere, only to be standing on the side of the building. I pray Isaac doesn't come outside.

****

Deb's neighbor, Marcy, decided to join us tonight. She's a party girl so it should be a fun night. The dance floor is filling up as the night flows on. This nightclub caters to everybody's tastes in music. All of it gets you moving, normally, but after two glasses of wine, I'm still wound up tight. At the insistence of Deb and Marcy, an intervention of serious alcohol is required, so a round of Vegas Bombs it will be.

The cover band's playing some kick ass music. A second round of Crown Royal, Red Bull, and their rendition of "Burn It to the Ground" drag my ass to the dance floor. Loosened up, the music takes over my body as it always does. A rhythmic movement in my right leg has my body slightly rockin'; my hips sway and my head bobbles around to the crescendo of the song. Bouncing and fist pumping, I lose myself to the music, joined by many bodies rocking in rhythm.

The music transfers from the band to the DJ. The dance

floor thins a little, but it's shoulder to shoulder line dancing and asses shaking; country girls following the song's request to shake it. The alcohol has slightly numbed my self-consciousness. I'm only periodically pulling on this short skirt barely covering my fat ass; my boobs bouncing in my corset. Sweat trickling down my back has forced me to come out of the sweater I wore to cover some of my exposed skin.

Deb and Marcy join me making a circle, dancing to ourselves. I feel hands on my hips and somebody grinding into my backside. I look back over my shoulder eyeing the top of greased back hair belonging to a man. The eyes of this head clearly watching his pelvis grind into my ass. I step forward to break the connection, but his grip tightens pulling me back into him.

****

Isaac

Bourbon has a nice smooth burn; the second shot going down is even better. It's so damn crowded in here. I fucking hate crowds. When I remodeled this warehouse it seemed huge at the time; now with all these people here, it appears very small.

I shouldn't be here. I should've stopped her at the club.

No... I'm trying to do the right thing, giving her space and keeping my head on straight. But she continues prodding and poking; the beast is clawing to get out.

Her waiting outside only antagonized my possessive feelings. *Where was she going? Who was she going with? Would she be safe?* I convince myself following her was for her safety. *Yeah, right.* I'll let her enjoy her night out. I'll just keep a watchful eye. Too many crazy people in this world.

It's been pretty easy to stay out of her sight with this crowd. She's staying pretty much at the table. Her and her friends are drinking a little too much to be out with no protection. *Fuck...she took her sweater off and she's heading to the dance floor.*

I'm kinda enjoying this. I have a better view of her and her delicious tits are bouncing. *My tits.* Her ass is swaying back and forth in perfect rhythm to the music. My cock is straining against my zipper. *My ass.*

Who the *FUCK* is that?

****

As his grip firms on my hips, my temper spikes. Squirming around to get enough room to jab my elbow in his gut, the hold on my hips is abruptly broken, replaced with a firm grip at the nape of my neck.

"This is *MINE*, motherfucker!" Growls past my ear. A menacing, inhuman voice with a vague familiarity to it.

My head immobile, I cut my eyes to see Isaac behind my shoulder. My peripheral vision catches a blur just as I'm shoved, stumbling backwards. A sickening cracking sound, focuses my attention to Isaac's fist colliding with the greaser's face, landing him on his back. I see Deb's look of utter shock and Marcy mouthing..." What the fuck?"

Grasping my neck once more, Isaac guides me through the crowd. I wrench my back turning toward him, sneering, to ask what the hell he's doing. The cold, fierceness of his eyes, has me thinking better of the situation, so I keep my mouth shut.

Jolting me back and forth, I can hardly put one foot in front of the other. He on the other hand, is weaving through the crowd with no resistance, almost like his rage is parting the way for him. If he wasn't gripping my neck, I would've faceplanted the floor already.

Finally off the dance floor, we continue down a hallway. Passing several closed doors, we come to a stop. "Control Room" is on the plate beside the door. *What the hell!* Without losing his hold on me, he opens the door and walks us both through the doorway. It's a small room with lots of computer stuff and electrical panels.

My ears are still roaring from the music pounding in the club, but I'm still able to hear the lock click on the door. He grabs my shoulders, shoving me against the wall. His hand cups around my chin. Fingers grip both sides, shaping my face into the likeness of a fish, forcing it upward to meet his glare. His other hand grapples under my skirt, palming my sex.

"This is *MINE*!" His breath laced with alcohol, hisses across my face. "No one keeps me from what's *MINE,* including you. No one touches what's *MINE*. I don't fucking share!"

My heart's pounding, I've never seen him like this. Trepidation intertwines with titillation. Thoughts of Vickie and the past two days melt away. My emotions are so confused...

He guides me over to a rectangular table.

"Bend over," he growls, pushing my back down.

My breasts flatten on the table. Most of my backside is

exposed in this position, but he yanks the bottom of my skirt up to my waist. Gripping my panties, he viciously jerks them, threads ripping under the pressure.

"You won't be needing these," he growls.

His hand flat between my shoulder blades, holding me firmly in place. My own heartbeat thrums in my ears. I vaguely hear a zipper, before feeling the head of his cock at my sex. My sex, that is drenched with need.

"Grab hold of the edge and don't let go," his commanding voice dropping an octave. *The Dom voice...* "This is for my pleasure, not yours. You have your safeword," he states, clearly a warning.

Grabbing my hips, he thrusts balls deep in my sex. I scream...not from pain, but shock and awe. He sets a pounding rhythm, grunting his possession.

"THIS IS MINE! YOU ARE MINE!" He roars with fierce determination.

The relentless pounding against that sweet spot within, drives my need to a quick, delicious eruption.

"OH MY GOD!" I scream with uncontrollable release, flowing down between my thighs.

Isaac removes his cock, running his fingers between my sodden folds, dragging my wetness over my puckered virgin hole. I clench down in fear. *Is he going to fuck my ass here???* He's fingered and played around with plugs, but he's never taken me there with his cock. His thick, thick cock. I shiver as his thumb penetrates my ass.

"Who do you belong to, Peaches? Whose ass is this?" His thumb circling just inside the rim of my ass, as his cock resumes thrusting deep in my sex.

"Who does this pussy belong to? ANSWER ME!" He roars.

"You... I belong to you," I sob.

"Damn right, you do."

Withdrawing once again, he flips me over to my back, dragging my ass over the edge of the table, sinking balls deep again.

Feverishly stroking in and out, he quickly pulls out. Shoving the bottom of my corset up, he groans as warm streams of his release streak across my stomach.

Leaning over me, Isaac runs his hands through his semen cooling on my skin, rubbing it into my stomach, my chest, and over my mound.

"You're covered in my scent. You belong to ME! Nobody fucking touches you but ME! Do you understand?"

"Yes, Master."

He gently tugs on my arms, helping me up. I stand, dumbfounded by what has just occurred. He straightens my corset and my skirt, as I just stand with my mouth gaping wide.

Taking my chin, gently this time, he lifts my gaze to his.

"You jumped to conclusions the other night and didn't give me a chance to explain. Then you shut me out. That will *NEVER* happen again. You will communicate with me; about everything. Are we clear?"

"Yes, Sir."

"That fucking bitch is nothing to me and I made myself very clear to her. I want to know if you ever hear from her again."

"Yes, Sir." *It's all I can say...yes, sir...yes, sir. My brain is malfunctioning.*

"I have fought to keep this dominant, possessive beast caged inside, hidden from you, but you tempted him one too many times. It's escaped and there's no turning back. I own you, now. You are MINE. We will discuss this further, at a later time. For now, go enjoy some time with your friends."

A kiss on my forehead...and he walks out the door.

What the hell just happened?!?!

Chapter 22

I take a few minutes to straighten my clothes and try to process what just happened. Slickness coats my inner thighs almost down to my knees. Thankfully a bathroom is across the hall, so I pop in there to clean up a bit. However, I'm only wiping off my thighs. I'm not touching Isaac's scent markings. I think it's HOT, in a sick, twisted kinda way.

A little more refreshed, I head down the hall to find Deb and Marcy. I hope they didn't ditch me here. *God, what they must be thinking...especially Marcy.* As I round the corner from the hallway, I see Isaac across the room talking to a man. Isaac shakes the man's hand, taps him on the shoulder, and walks toward the door. *Eeeww...I hope Isaac washed his hands.*

I see Deb and Marcy sitting at our table and I head that way. *Thank God they didn't leave me.* Deb leaps off the stool and intercepts me just before I get to the table.

"God, Kathy...are you okay? Where's Isaac?" Deb pants out.

"I'm fine...I think. Isaac left."

"What happened? He looked like he could rip somebody apart."

"Let's just say he wanted to clarify our relationship."

"Huh...what?" Deb's face contorts in confusion.

"An ownership fuck...yep, that's what I call it," I muse.

"Oh..." Deb chuckles.

I've had enough fun, so we call it a night. Deb drives me over to Nexus to pick up my car. It's late and I'm exhausted, so I use my spare key. I'll get my other key from Isaac later. The last two days have seemed like an eternity. I'm physically exhausted and emotionally drained. I can't get home fast enough.

Finally home, I drop my stuff by the door. I hear Max scratching on one of the bedroom doors. I love when the guys are home, but they throw me out of my routine. Whoever was here last, didn't set the alarm and accidentally shut Max up in one of the bedrooms. Down the hallway, I hear the scratching coming from Matt's room. *Big shocker, he's not the most observant kid...*

From the darkness of the hall, a sweaty hand clamps

over my mouth and I feel a prickle at my neck. Panic seizes my heart.

"I'm gonna have a little fun with you, bitch!"

The voice is gravelly and the breath wreaks of alcohol and stale cigarettes. My mind races with everything I've ever read or been told to do, in case of an attack. Fight or flight... Fight or submit... *I only submit to one man.*

"Don't scream and I'll move my hand. Scream and I'll cut ya."

I nod in compliance. I mentally try to size him up, strategizing a way to escape. He's taller than me, but not has tall as Isaac.

He starts pulling me toward my bedroom in a semi choke hold and I start scrambling toward Matt's door. Max is going crazy trying to get out. My heart is beating out of my chest.

I'm jerked backwards and in a split second decision, I throw my head back with the momentum. Hoping to hit him in the nose or mouth, like Isaac taught me – go *for the weak points*, my head rams into his throat. *I'll take that.* My attacker releases his hold on me. Bringing his hands to his throat, a burning streaks across my upper arm. I lunge forward, losing my balance, landing on the floor. He's still gasping for air and I struggle up to my knees grasping for Matt's door handle. I feel warmth oozing down my arm to my neck, realizing he has cut me in the struggle. Fingertips barely on the handle, the grip is just enough to open the door when I pull down on the handle.

A growling blur leaps over my head. Growling, gnawing and shrieking yells fill the air. I look back and see Max with a firm hold on the intruder's arm. That's when I notice the intruder wearing a mask. I spot the knife on the floor and grab it before scrambling to my feet. I stagger down the hallway, while Max remains in control. Though he's a hundred pound German Shepherd, Max can only stave the intruder off for so long.

I hear Max yelp just as I hit the panic button on the security system. The alarm pierces through the night. Max is still gnawing and growling, but a larger commotion begins. The intruder is on his feet, fighting Max off as he backs down the hallway. New fear emerges. With no time to act, I find some unknown courage deep within and decide to attack the intruder with his knife.

Not wanting to get trapped in the hall again, I wait till he gets to the end of it. Poised to lunge at his back, I'm shocked when he turns and bolts out the door. Max standing guard between me and the door, I collapse to the floor while the mélange of alarms and sirens surround us.

After what seems like forever, but truly only a few minutes, a loud rapping on the door startles me and Max begins a barrage of fierce barking at the door.

"POLICE...put your hands where we can see them!"

A male voice shouts, a voice I recognize. *Patrick...* I exhale the breath I've been holding. The door kicks open and Patrick stands with his gun drawn, pointing directly at me and Max. Two uniformed officers stand behind him, guns pointing in the same direction.

"Call the dog down!" Yells one of the uniformed officers.

"Max...come," I meekly call.

Max hesitates, but the hair on his back lays down and slowly he comes to me. I wrap my arms around him and he licks my face. His way of making sure I'm okay.

"Jeezus...Katherine," Patrick sighs, stroking the top of my head.

"Call for an ambulance...she has a laceration on her arm," Patrick calls out to the other officer. "Check the bathroom for a towel or something, to wrap around her arm."

"Are you *hurt*...anywhere else?" Patrick asks continuing to stroke my hair.

I understand his insinuation, knowing in my heart, the vilest act I can imagine would've happened to me, if it weren't for Max.

"No...," I murmur, still trembling in my skin.

"Shhh, you're safe now, Katherine. I'm gonna call Isaac."

****

Isaac

I should've made her leave with me; this would've never happened. *Master*...I'm no fucking master. My job is to protect her, but instead she's ambushed in her own home. *God, is she okay?*

Motherfucking prick wouldn't tell me anything on the phone... '*Someone broke in Katherine's house; she was home. You need to get over here...*', then he hangs up the phone.

What the fuck kinda shit is that?

Gas pedal on the floor, I can't get there fast enough. *Fuck...she lives too far away!*

As I drive down her street, red and blue lights entertain the neighbors standing in their yards. I can't even get to her house for police cars, ambulance, and rescue trucks. *Ambulance...*

I jump out of my truck and bolt across the yard toward her front door. Someone clotheslines my chest and grabs my arm. Fist cocked, I pivot around and catch a glimpse of Pat's face just in time, keeping me from smashing it in.

"Whoa, Isaac...hang on a minute."

"Where is she? Is she okay?"

"She's inside."

"I need to see her. What the fuck happened, Pat?"

"Calm down... They're talking to her. I called in a female officer. I thought she would be more comfortable talking to a female, than me."

"What *HAPPENED* to her?" I growl, rage beginning to rumble in my gut.

"She came home and someone was already in the house. Snuck up behind her. She fought... She head-butted him in larynx, giving her a chance to let the dog out. Her German Shepherd held the intruder off long enough for her to hit the panic button on her house alarm. During the struggle, she sustained a laceration on her upper arm."

"Laceration? He had a fucking knife?" I ask, rage nearly boiling over.

"Katherine said he had the knife at her throat dragging her to her bedroom; that's when she head-butted him. During her struggle to get away, the knife came across her arm.

I was patrolling a few blocks away, when the call came over the radio. I didn't know Katherine lived in this neighborhood. Imagine my shock seeing her when I kicked the door in."

I need to know... I want to ask..., but I can't find the words to communicate. My mind doesn't want to go there. My concern must be plastered all over my face.

"She said she wasn't *hurt* anywhere else," Pat confirms, alleviating my fears. "I called in the female officer, just to be sure."

Sighing a huge relief, a female officer approaches Pat

and he steps away to speak with her.

"Katherine confirmed to Officer Adams that a sexual assault did not occur," Pat explains.

That tidbit of info calms my fear and tampers the rage, somewhat. Pat gives me the all clear to go in to see Katherine.

I step into the living room and she's sitting on the sofa, arm bandaged, and the dog sitting beside her. As I approach, she looks up and a single tear streaks her right cheek. She steps into my open arms, burying her face in my chest. I stroke her back and her trembling begins to ease.

"I'm so sorry baby girl. I should've been here," I whisper into her hair.

"He saved my life. Max saved my life," She whispers into my chest, her warm breath seeping through my shirt.

"How's your arm? Do you need to go to the ER?"

"No ER. The cut's not deep, it's superficial. The paramedics put adhesive and steri-strips along the cut to keep it closed."

She pulls away from my chest, looking toward the kicked in front door.

"I need to call Debra to see if I can stay with her until I can get the front door fixed. Are the police responsible for paying for their damages?" She rambles.

"You will be going home with me. I'll come over tomorrow and fix the door. Security upgrades will be made to your house before you stay here again," I grouse.

"I can't stay with you. Ben leaves for France in a few days and I have tons to do before then. He's in and out, Matt's in and out...I never know when they're home during the summer. I can't leave Max here by himself," panic laces her voice.

"We'll come over for you to get some things done, but Ben's a grown man and I'm sure he can take care of some of his travel needs. The guys being in and out so much, is exactly why you will be staying with me until I check out all the doors and windows in this house. Now, as far as Max, he'll come with us. Problem solved."

"I can't impose on you with Max, too. I'll..."

"Enough...it's settled," I interrupt her jabber.

Chapter 23

Blinking the sleep from my eyes, I try to orientate myself to my surroundings. Reality dawns and memories from last night flood through my mind. *Shit... someone broke into my home and tried to attack me.* I shiver...

An arm clamped across my chest, a hand palming my right breast, and my nipple being rolled and pulled by a thumb and finger.

"Morning, baby," Isaac whispers, kissing the back of my neck while his cock twitches at the crease of my ass.

"Good Morning, Sir," I murmur, squirming my ass against his cock.

A light smack lands on my left butt cheek...

"Keep that ass still. You need to remember who's in charge," he grumbles in my ear.

With everything that happened last night, I was so wound up I couldn't sleep. Isaac and I talked about our previous marriages and how they had skewed our views of relationships; in different ways. His wife being unfaithful with someone he considered a friend; blaming Isaac for smothering her with his control. That caused his emotions to shut down and he withdrew emotionally from everyone. Him opening up and sharing his past, helps me understand his views about us and the new direction of our relationship. Fortunately, our views are similar, as well as our expectations of each other. His need for control, his possessiveness; which I believe is the way a relationship is supposed to be. I belong to him and he belongs to me. We respect ourselves and each other. Honesty and communication...

Communicating... I shared with Isaac the events from the Chicago trip. So much has happened since I got back, I haven't had a chance to tell him.

He reined in his anger better than I thought he would. I think he was being considerate of me and everything that has happened. I experienced the gentler side to Isaac. Sometimes, making love slow and sweet, is what's needed most. Even though "I'll kill that motherfucker if he touches you again" is being whispered like sweet nothings in my ear.

"You're in charge, Sir," I smile as arms tighten around me.

"That's right, baby," he groans, circling my clit with his finger.

"This is my pussy and my tits," he declares, slowly driving his cock into my pussy, while pulling and twisting my nipples.

He continues his gradual assault: caressing my clit, nibbling and biting my shoulder, while stroking in and out of my pussy. Skyrocketing my need for release.

"Please Sir...I need to come," I quietly beg.

Stroking in and out a few more times, Isaac sinks his teeth into my shoulder, squeezing my clit at the same time.

"Aaagghhhh..." An animalistic scream roars from my soul.

With no recoup, he smacks my ass... "Hands and knees, Peaches."

I quickly present to him and he positions himself behind me. A dollop of cold gooeyness oozes its way between the cheeks of my ass. I cringe...

"Who do you belong to, Peaches?"

"You, Sir. I belong to you."

"That's right. And I've claimed every part of you...except the one part that no one ever has. This sweet, beautiful ass," he says with a sinister laugh. "It's all MINE."

I clench every orifice I have, including the tight virgin hole that Isaac wants to *explore*. Every muscle in my body is in lockdown mode. I'm trembling in fear and apprehension. I want to please him, but I'm so fucking scared. *That's a small hole for his thick cock. It's gonna hurt...*

I feel the head of his cock spreading the ooze around my ass. His thumb easily penetrates the rim and he begins massaging my ass in a circular motion. *Shit... he's really gonna do this*. He caresses his hand up and down my back to calm my jitters.

"It's okay, baby. I'm gonna make you feel so good. You're gonna love it. You'll be begging me to fuck this sweet little ass, again and again. I promise..."

He's out of his fucking mind, if he really believes that...

"I need you to relax for me, Peaches. Take a deep breath. I'm gonna take care of you."

Isaac removes his thumb and I feel the head of his cock at the rim of my ass. He gradually eases his cock in. *FUCK... it burns*. I clench my ass as tight as I can.

Slapping my ass cheek he growls, "Relax and open up for me, Peaches. This ass belongs to me."

"I can't!" I growl back.

Expecting another swat, instead he draws his fingers up and down my spine like a feather.

"I'm going to move slow, Peaches. It burns a little at first, but I promise it will transform into ecstasy for you. Remember...immense pleasure is born from a little pain. You always have your safeword, baby."

I take a deep breath... trying to relax.

"I'm ready, Sir..."

I feel more cold goo and then he positions his cock once again at my ass. He reaches around and begins rubbing my clit. I immediately begin to relax. Taking advantage of my arousal, he penetrates the head of his cock through the rim of my ass. I wince, sucking air between clenched teeth.

His cock stills, as he continues fingering my clit. He eases out of my burning hole and right back in; inching deeper. Methodically, he continues this process. Nerve endings I've never felt, suddenly ignite a wildfire in my core. My pussy begins throbbing with need. With every withdrawal, he drives deeper and deeper until I feel his balls flush with my cheeks. He stills...

"That's my *good girl.*"

Beads of sweat dot my forehead and I'm panting... How can something so wrong...so taboo... feel so unimaginably delicious. The sensations in my ass are dousing the throbbing flames of need, with gasoline. I'm about to spontaneously combust. I don't recognize the growling sounds coming from within me.

"Hold on baby... I'm gonna send you soaring," He groans... so fucking sexy.

He begins a slow progression of thrusts; in and out. Sparks of white heat explode behind my eyes. I'm rapidly ascending to the precipice; the point of losing all control. His thrusts drive me higher and higher. My body trembles, as I free fall into ecstasy.

I'm soaring, floating above all that is life. I feel giddy and tingly all over. This is utter Bliss...

I barely register the guttural roar from Isaac upon his release. It's just enough to anchor my ascension. I hover in my blissful state...

****

God, I hope I'm not walking as bow-legged as I feel. My ass is still a little sore from Isaac's *exploration* yesterday. Hell, my entire body aches from the assault Saturday night. I ignored Isaac's requests to stay home from work today to recuperate. He told me the soreness would be worse today and he was right, but we have some damage control to perform today at work. Rick's shenanigans in Chicago nearly cost us a multimillion dollar account. I hope he's not in this meeting with Rob this morning, it will be awkward.

I'm the first one in the conference room, so I take a seat. I squirm about to find a position that alleviates some of the residual burning and soreness in my ass. Each twinge reminds me of the wicked pleasure Isaac inflicted, causing my sex to twitch. *He was right...I want him to take me, my ass, like that again. Damn him...*

The door opening brings my attention back to the conference room, as the others file in the room. *No Rick...Thank goodness!*

Rob makes a conference call to Mr. Douglas, for us all to hear. Rob explains to Mr. Douglas that Rick was given a week off, without pay, for his reckless conduct in Chicago. Mr. Douglas wants him fired but Rob explains that his behavior occurred in a social setting, and not while he was on the clock. He also confirmed that Rick has been taken off the Syntec ad team and to my surprise, Rob will be handling the account personally for the foreseeable future. That bit of news has lightened Mr. Douglas's mood. Rob ends the call and we settle in, bringing Rob up to speed on the account.

Back at my desk, I'm about to plunge into reworking the Syntec files, when Jean's voice startles me.

"You have a visitor, Katherine. So I thought I would escort him to you," Jean says gleefully.

I look up into Isaac's handsomely, rugged face and warm chestnut eyes.

"Hey, babe. I was in the area and thought you might want to have lunch," he says with deviousness dancing in his eyes.

My gaze pans back and forth between him, smiling like the cat that swallowed the canary and Jean beaming from ear to ear.

"Well, are you gonna introduce us?" Jean asks, still smiling with a gleam in her eye.

"Of course... Jean, this is Isaac, my..." *Hell, what is he? My boyfriend, my Master, my Sir??? What the hell am I supposed to say???*

"Man...I'm her man," Isaac interrupts, smiling. *Mmmm, Dimples...*

"Well, hello Isaac. It's a pleasure to meet you," Jean oozes, offering her hand.

"Likewise..." Isaac utters, bringing Jean's hand to his lips.

I think for a moment, Jean is going to faint. She has that goo-goo look in her eyes.

"You okay, Jean?" I giggle.

"Uh, yes. I'm good. I need to get back to work, though. Enjoy lunch," Jean winks as she walks away.

Stepping around my desk, I place my hands on his hips and he wraps his arms around me. I'm surrounded with his sinfully musky scent.

"And to what do I owe this surprise visit?" Standing on my tippy toes to place a soft kiss on his lips.

"Told ya. I was in the area and thought we could have

lunch."

"Uh-huh."

"And I wanted to see how my girl is feeling today."

"That's sweet. I'm a little achy all over, but not too bad."

"So, where's this prick...Rick. Where's his desk?"

I know good and damn well why he's here. Staking his claim...sending a visual warning to Rick.

"His desk is on the other side of the building."

"Hmm...maybe you can take me on a tour of the building," he grouses.

"No need, Rick's not here. I found out this morning that he was suspended for a week without pay."

"Little prick's lucky that's all he got. I'll break him, if he even looks at you the wrong way again."

I smile into his hardened face, "Come on, honey. Let's go to lunch."

Chapter 24

Summer is flying by. It's been almost two months since the break-in and no arrest has been made. There's been very few leads, however there hasn't been another break-in or assault linked to the case, since mine occurred.

Isaac kept his word and did an overhaul of the entryways to the house. Replacing the door jams with reinforced steel frames, new dead bolts, and window locks. It feels like I'm at Fort Knox. Though I spend most of my time at Isaac's, if I stay here, Isaac stays here, too.

Ben arrived home from France yesterday and he and Matt are heading back to college next week, so a little family get together tonight is in order.

Isaac has taken Max on their weekly ride in the country. Max loves riding in the back of the truck. Isaac spoils that dog, taking him to the meat market to get a fresh bone every Saturday.

****

It was wishful thinking that the boys would stick around very long after dinner; people to see and places to go.

Comfy on the sofa, curled up in Isaac's arms, I'm chomping at the bit, waiting for the right time to talk to him about a situation with work. *Guess there's no time like the present...*

"Umm, I need to talk to you about something," I mumble.

"I'm all ears, babe."

"Well, I...umm..."

"Spit it out, girl..."

"I have a business trip to Memphis next week."

"Okay. And..."

"Rick's going on the trip," I wince.

I hear a low growl deep in his chest. We have discussed the many facets of our relationship; expectations and guidelines. His control does not cross over into my professional life. However, this is a very unique situation that I need his input on.

The silence lingers.

"I haven't had any issues with him since the Chicago incident. I think the suspension had a positive effect on him." I explain.

"I don't like it," he groans in my ear. "I understand it's your job, but I fucking don't like it."

"I can ask to be removed from the project."

"I won't ask you to do that."

"I think he'll be fine. I really do."

"How long will you be gone?"

"I leave Wednesday and return early Thursday morning. I would come back Wednesday night, but I have a dinner meeting Wednesday evening."

His arms tighten around me. I sneak a peek up at him and see the worry in his face. Knowing what I do about his past and his needs, I understand the internal struggle he's having. He doesn't want to interfere with my job, but he wants to protect me.

"Can you take a few days off for a long weekend?" He asks out of the blue.

"I have some vacation time. Why?"

"The Blue Angels are having an Air Show in Pensacola next weekend. It's been years since I've seen them. I think you'd like it. We could stay in Perdido Key. It's a secluded island near Pensacola."

"That sounds awesome!"

"I can drive to Hendersonville Wednesday morning to check on the jobsite there, and then I can meet you in Memphis Wednesday night. Hendersonville is about three and a half hours from Memphis. We can head out early Thursday morning. Save your boss some money on your return flight."

"That would be perfect, Sir. You wouldn't be too far away," I beam with excitement. "Were you stationed at Pensacola when you were in the Navy?"

"I was stationed at Gulfport, but it's only two hours from Pensacola, so I went to the airshows when I got a chance."

"Oh Sir...I'm so excited! Our first trip together, I can't wait!!!"

****

Of course, the days went slowly by, but Wednesday finally arrived. The excitement of Isaac and my first trip together, overshadows any apprehension and dread I have about the business trip with Rick. I will keep my distance from him.

The day has gone very well. The dinner meeting was very successful and now it's transitioned into a social event. To my dismay, Rick has fallen into his pattern of consuming hefty amounts of alcohol and is being quite boisterous. Thankfully, this will be an early evening for me. Isaac will be here later tonight.

I check my phone and see a voicemail notification. I excuse myself from the group, in search of quiet place to check my voicemail.

Just as I thought, Isaac left a message saying he was on his way. Checking the time, I estimate he should be here around 10pm. I head back toward our table and I hear Rick's loud mouth before I turn the corner. Deciding not to stick around to witness the train wreck that is Rick, I bid my goodnights and head to my room.

Showered and dressed in my T-shirt and panties, I curl

up on the bed to read, waiting for Isaac. Loud knocking on the door startles me. *Isaac made it here quicker than I thought.* I scramble off the bed, literally bouncing to the door. *Funny how being in a hotel makes you all giddy and excited.*

"Hey there!" I exclaim, swinging the door wide open.

My heart seizes when Rick is standing in the doorway. Stunned still...it finally dawns on me I'm standing in my shirt and panties.

"Well hey to you...," he slurs.

"What are you doing here?" I screech pulling on the bottom of my shirt. I step back to close the door some, so I can stand behind it.

Rick puts his forearm on the door, bracing like he thinks I'm going to slam the door on him. *Good guess...*

"I was looking for you downstairs. Why'd you leave so early?"

"I have any early day tomorrow."

He pushes his way on in, the bottom of the door skimming across the tops of my toes. *SHIT...that hurt!!!* I stagger a bit, bumping into the wall, trying to protect the rest of my toes.

"Look, Rick...you need to leave," I state firmly.

"Ah, come on...the nights young," he boasts swinging his arms around walking farther in the room, toward the bed.

Isaac will go ballistic if he finds Rick in this room. I think he would seriously hurt him. Rick has to leave now. I need to reason with him. *Right...reason with a drunk. Good luck.* I walk toward him and grasp his elbow.

"Seriously Rick, you need to leave. I'm expecting someone."

The goofy, inebriated look on his face is quickly replaced with a sinister glare.

"Yeah, right," he smirks, jerking his arm away.

"Rick you're drunk and not thinking straight. You're going to mess around and lose your job. Please just leave. I don't want to call security, but I will."

He shoves me back on the bed and climbs on top of me.

"What the fuck are you doing?" I begin flailing my fists around like a person gone mad. I begin to scream and he puts some cloth material in my mouth. Panic grips my heart as I can't get enough air in through my nose. I need to calm down or I'm going to pass out. I'm still punching, bucking, tossing;

trying to throw him off balance.

"You're not going to call anybody," he snarks, ripping the phone from the wall.

He maneuvers his knees across the tops of my arms, making them immobile. The cloth is loose in my mouth and I work my tongue and jaws frantically trying to get it out.

"Expecting someone. Ha...that's a joke. Who the fuck's coming to see you? Nobody, that's who. You should be thanking me, baby. I'm gonna give you a good, hard fucking. I know it's probably been a long time for you. Not many men line up to fuck fat chicks, right?" He roars laughter.

Stupid fuck...rage erupts in my soul. During his delusional rant, I'm able to work the cloth free. At least enough for me to breathe and talk.

"Jesus Rick, don't do this," I plea.

"I'm gonna give it to you just like you want it. See...I know you've been going to that sex club; dressing like a slut. I wouldn't have guessed you like it rough and kinky, or are you that desperate? It's okay though...I like it rough, too."

How does he know about Nexus? He must've followed me there. Shit...he's been stalking me.

"I know you've been checking me out, thinking I wouldn't be interested cause your fat. Now, I'm no chubby chaser, but I do like a variety," He snorts.

I feel him wrapping something around my wrist. *No, No, No...* Now the other, oh God, please help me! He moves his knees, momentarily freeing one arm while he pulls the cable on the other wrist toward the edge of the bed. I pummel his back and head as hard as I can, trying to gain some leverage. Colors explode behind my eyes as I catch a blow to the side of my face.

Woozy and dazed, I shake my head to clear my thoughts. Then I realize my arms are bound above my head and I'm gagged again.

"See what you made me do? Let's ease into it, Katherine. We'll gradually get to rough stuff," he snorts again, crawling back on top of me straddling my chest. *Shit...I can't breathe.*

He slaps my face twice, but nowhere near as hard as the blow to my head. Tears fill my eyes from the sting, a metallic taste seeping through the cloth, between my lips.

"You like that, bitch!" He spits at me, slapping me across the face again. "I didn't know I would like this. Maybe I should check out that sex club. This shit gets me hard," slapping me again. *He's fucking crazy...*

Every slap causes me to pull on the cord, cutting into my wrists. *Isaac...please get here soon. PLEASE!!!*

I can't get enough air in through my nose for my lungs to expand. I'm scared I'm going to hyperventilate and pass out, leaving me completely at Rick's mercy, or lack thereof. Garnering all my strength, I push my feet into the bed, trying to buck him off of me. It only earns me a backhand across my face; the taste of copper seeps between my lips.

A quick session of knocks on the door halts the slapping. *Isaac....*

"Go the fuck away!" Rick hollers out. "We're busy."

"Katherine!" Isaac yells through the door.

I try to make as much noise as possible with the gag in my mouth. Two thuds on the door and it crashes open. Rick's not off of me fast enough...I hear a roar and Rick's gone from my sight. I hear a sickening crack and splatter.

Isaac is instantly at my side. He removes my gag and works to free my wrists and ankles. Drawing me up in his arms.

"FUCK!!! Baby...are you okay?"

Sobbing into his chest, I can only nod.

"I'm gonna kill that motherfucker!" He roars.

Isaac bolts from the bed and lifts Rick like a ragdoll, viciously pounding his face. Dropping him to the ground, Isaac stomps and kicks him repeatedly. The cracking and popping is making me sick.

"POLICE! Hands in the air!" Two officers yell from the doorway.

"I'll fucking kill him if he touches her again." Isaac threatens.

"Sir...step away. Let us handle from here."

Isaac hesitantly backs away from Rick's limp, broken body piled on the floor and moves over to sit by me on the bed.

Isaac wraps me in his arms and holds me tight against him. *I never want to leave his embrace. I feel so safe here. I replay the events involving Rick over the last few months. I should've listened to my gut. I should've reported him. Others should've reported his sexual advances. We all felt sorry for his wife...his children. He's got serious issues.*

"I love you... My god Katherine, I love you. I can't lose you, baby."

Isaac's words stun me at first, then warmth radiates through my body. *He loves me. He said it...he loves me.*

"I love you, Isaac...so much I think my heart will burst!" I snuggle further into his chest. *I feel so safe in his arms.*

"Babe, did he...did he...touch...violate you...*there*?" Isaac struggles to get the words out.

"N-no... just hit me," I stammer.

"Baby, I promise... I'll keep you safe from now on."

"He knows I go to Nexus...he followed me," I whisper into Isaac's chest. "He said he saw me dressed like a slut. I should've listened to you...listened to my gut." I sob.

"Sshhh... You need to tell the police everything, babe."

I nod and wrap my arms tighter around Isaac. *How can something like this happen to a person...twice?* Gently rocking me in his arms, Isaac suddenly stops. Shifting me and propping me against the headboard of the bed, he stands approaching the chaotic scene around Rick on the floor.

"Hey...can you check his arms for scars or puncture

wounds?" Isaac calls out to the paramedics.

"Excuse me...," one of the medics replies quizzically.

"Scars or puncture marks...does that prick have any on his arm?" Isaac surly repeats. "It could be relevant to this case."

Scars or puncture marks? What in the world is Isaac thin-??? Oh, no. No, no!!!

"Near the elbow, on the right arm, there are several healed puncture marks. They are asymmetrical; a tearing of the skin similar to an animal bite," the medic explains.

"Oh my god," I gasp in realization of how bizarre this situation has just become.

Chapter 25

Sliding the black lace stocking over my right knee, coming to rest mid-thigh, I stand and turn toward the mirror to assess the vertical cross pattern centered down the back of my leg. It appears three times' a charm on the right leg, after getting it perfect the first time on the left. I attach the silk straps dangling from the black lace garter belt. Shimmying into the black satin skirt, thankfully made with Lycra, I step back to get a full frontal view of the ensemble. The purple lace trim on the bottom of the skirt matches my corset perfectly. I thought it was fitting to wear the same corset I wore my first night at Nexus, to my collaring ceremony.

Honor, Love, Trust, Devotion, and Communication are the founding elements in a D/s relationship. Since learning about the significance of collaring, it resembles marriage in many ways and for many couples, it replaces marriage vows.

It's been a month since the attack in Memphis and Rick's subsequent arrest. He was charged with assault, breaking and entering my home, as well as stalking;

however, no connection has been made between Rick and the other assaults and break-ins.

Since then, Isaac has been resolved to move forward in our relationship. I have officially moved in with him, though I'm keeping my house. The collaring is to signify our relationship to our friends, family, and the Nexus community. His possessive need being met.

Bags packed, I'm super excited we're finally taking our trip to Florida; the one thwarted after the incident in Memphis. I hate Isaac missed the Air Show. He was really looking forward to seeing the Blue Angels, but I'm thrilled to be getting away together. Kind of a honeymoon for collaring... a *Submoon.*

Happy to have a moment alone to reflect, a reel of memories flutter through my mind while walking down the stairs to the club. My thoughts linger on the vision of seeing Isaac for the first time...

Towering around 6' 3", wearing black slacks, black dress shirt - barely containing his brawny physique. The rugged, chiseled features of his face surrounded by short, chestnut colored hair with a sprinkling of grey at his temple. Dimples hidden within a 5 o'clock shadow, outlining his strong jawline, an Adonis.

Oh my... just the thought of him makes my sex hum. I open the door and Patrick is waiting in the hall, my escort to join Isaac.

"You look stunning, Katherine."

"Thank you, Master Patrick," I murmur nervously.

Patrick takes my left hand, wrapping it around his elbow.

"You're trembling, girl. You having second thoughts," Patrick chuckles to lighten the mood.

"I've never been more sure of anything. I'm just a little nervous. I don't want to goof up and embarrass myself or Isaac."

"Ha...I don't think you have to worry about that. However, if his senses take a leave of absence, just give me a wink and a nod. I'll knock him on his ass and take his place."

Patrick's warm and hearty laughter calms my jitters.

We stroll down the hall, around the corner into the heart of Nexus, we pause and I soak up the atmosphere. Derek, Gina, Zeke, Tiny – the entire Nexus staff, are all here. Charlotte and Edward, as well as several other members of the club, all in attendance too. Of course, this wouldn't be happening without the insistence of Debra for a girls' night out. I'm so happy she's here tonight. My eyes continue to pan across the room, finally resting on my Adonis...Isaac.

Dressed completely in black, his sun-kissed skin is the perfect canvas for his chestnut eyes. His gaze draws me to him and I kneel at his feet. Though Isaac doesn't request this from me, I honor the ceremonious tradition.

Patrick begins a welcome speech for our guests, but I can't focus on anything but Isaac. I'm drowning in the warmth of his eyes. He strokes down my cheek as I begin my vow.

"Master Isaac, I kneel before you offering my heart, my body, and my soul. My love and devotion belong to you and you alone. All of me I give to you...to love, honor, and protect." A steady stream of tears streak down my cheeks.

Expecting a leather collar, I gasp in surprise when Isaac removes a beautiful silver and gold entwined choker from a black velvet pouch.

"Katherine, I'm honored to accept your precious gifts. I will keep your heart in mine, protecting it with every ounce of my being. I will cherish every inch of your body. I will merge your soul within my own. You belong to me and I to you. I love you, honor you and will protect you with my dying breath. This collar is a symbol of my love, devotion, and protection. It's removal only at my hand."

Isaac places the beautiful collar around my neck, while tears continue to flow. He gathers my hands in his, guiding me to my feet. My body's trembling so, I can hardly stand. Isaac places his lips softly on mine, encouraging my lips to part, allowing him to explore. I lose myself in his embrace.

He pulls away from his smoldering kiss and drops to one knee. Confusingly, I stare down at Isaac, trying to figure out what in the world he's doing, when the sight of Ben and Matt catch my attention.

"Wha-wha- what are you doing here?" I stammer, eyes bugging out of my head. *Why in the hell are my sons here...at Nexus?* They just stand there smiling back at me, not saying a word.

Isaac takes my hand, "Katherine...you wearing my collar means the world to me. I meant each and every word of my vow to you. My world was dark and cold before your light shone into my soul, thawing my frozen heart. I didn't believe love existed...at least not for me, not until you walked into my life. As you can see, Ben and Matt are here and I've spoken with them, about my feelings for you. I love you, Katherine and I want to spend the rest of my life with you. Will you marry me?"

Tremors wrack my body and my vision blurs the colors of the spectrum. I blink away the tears, focusing on the stunning diamond sparkling before my eyes. It's absolutely gorgeous. I snag a glance at the boys standing off to the side, they're both beaming.

I can't believe this is really happening...Isaac just asked me to marry him. Oh my god...

"Yes... Yes...I will marry you."

The room erupts with applause and Isaac lifts me off my feet, assaulting my lips with a deliciously, possessive kiss. Matt and Ben approach as Isaac releases his hold on me. They surround me in a group hug.

"Mom, we just want you to be happy," Ben kisses me on the cheek.

"And we know Isaac makes you happy," Matt chimes in.

"Thank you, guys. It means a lot to know you accept my decision. I love you both so very much!"

Skinny arms wrap around my neck, squeezing tight and squeals of delight fill my ears.

"Oh my god, Kathy. I can't believe you're getting married," Deb shrills in my ear.

"I know, I know, I know...," I squeal jumping all around.

Isaac grabs me in an embrace, while our friends and family surround us offering their congratulations.

"So it seems I didn't need to knock him on his ass after all," Patrick chuckles. "Just my luck."

Shaking my head, "Oh Patrick..." I laugh back at him.

Overwhelmed with excitement, I take a minute to absorb all the laughter and warm wishes. I notice Deb standing off to the side with an awestruck look on her face. I follow her gaze lingering on Patrick. *Time to play a little matchmaking...*

"Patrick, do you remember my friend Debra?"

"How could I forget that little yellow dress? Long time no see, Sunshine. We need to get you back to the club more often," Patrick oozes in that sexy voice of his. Deb just stands there drooling, like a love sick school girl.

I make my way back over to my man and he wraps me in his arms.

I've read many romance novels but I never dreamed I could find someone to love me the way the heroines were loved in my favorite books.

I'm right where I need to be...in the arms of the man that awakened my desires and make all my dreams come true.

The End

Next in the Nexus Series

SOLEIL – The Nexus Series #2

Synopsis

Divorced and settled into single life, Debra planned a "Girls Night Out" to rival all, arranging a visit to Nexus, a local BDSM club, for her best friend Katherine. To their surprise, Katherine catches the eye of the club owner, Isaac, igniting a scorching hot connection that has led to their engagement.

Though she loved her visit to Nexus, Debra has shunned her friend's invitations to become a member, feeling she would be a third wheel to the engaged couple. Then fate intervenes and Debra gets an invitation to Nexus from someone she can't deny.

In her mid-forties, Debra is on the verge of experiencing a life she never realized she desired. Her new found erotic fantasies have her exploring life's most taboo behaviors with not one, but two Alpha males who have stolen her heart. Throwing caution to the wind, Debra embarks on a journey to find love, which could ultimately lead to the destruction of her heart.

Believing she's found the road to happiness, guilt and shame consume her when a tragic loss thrusts her ex-husband back into her life, dredging up regrets of the past.

Will Debra embrace the new life she's discovered at Nexus, or will she allow old feelings and close-minded ideals, to derail her happiness and a chance at love?

DECEIT – The Nexus Series #3

Synopsis:
Gina's been drawn to the dark and mysterious Leo, since the moment he first returned to Nexus. However, her sordid past prevents from offering her complete submission.

Leo put up a good fight, but Gina's natural submissiveness taunts his sadistic nature. Leo demands open and honest communication, something Gina struggles with.

Can Gina endure Leo's demanding ways or will her past destroy her and those closest to her, including newlyweds, Katherine and Isaac?

WICKED ~ The Nexus Series #4

CHARLOTTE and EDWARD

You know them.

You envy them.

You secretly crave to be WITH them.

They are WICKED!

Discover the lascivious and tantalizing journey of Charlotte and Edward and how they became the Dynamic Duo of Nexus.

Other publications by Lainie Suzanne

BLOOD MOON ~ An Erotic Vampire Novella

Erotic-Lust ~ Vengeance ~ Immortality

Synopsis:

Love fades. Immortality is forever. ~ Unknown

Two years ago, Melaina Harrison's boyfriend was killed in an accident and her life has been in a rut since. Each day merging into the next. Then one fateful night, a dark and seductive stranger walks into her life and shifts her world off its axis. Her new lover's incredible perception of her wants and desires has her reeling in ecstasy; as if he knows her every thought.

Keres Re is beautiful, intelligent, strong; the epitome of the perfect woman. The perfect vampire. Men fall at her feet, both vampire and human. What more could a woman want? Keres wants what all women want, the love of her life. She found her eternal love, however Andrew died in a tragic accident before Keres had a chance to capture his heart for forever. The death she blames on one person – Melaina Harrison.

For two years, Keres has plotted and formulated a plan to avenge the death of her intended eternal lover. She enlists the help of her brother Marco to execute her vengeance.

Will Melaina discover her lover's true existence or will Keres enact her revenge?

About the Author

Lainie Suzanne is from Atlanta, Georgia and makes her home in North Carolina. She's married to her best friend and the love of her life. The mother of four, all flown from the nest, she and her husband share their home with their German Shepherd. She loves sports, listening to music, dancing, spending time with family, and of course...reading.

Find Lainie Suzanne on Social Media:

Facebook
Twitter
Pinterest
Google+
Goodreads
Instagram
Tsu
www.lainiesuzanne.com

Printed in Great Britain
by Amazon